N~st~
to~
lan~scapes and a warm, ~~~~ ~~~~~~~ ~~munit~ it is ~
lucky tourist who stumbles upon this little h~ven.

But n~~ Mills & Boon® Medical™ Romance is giving readers the unique opportunity to visit this fictional coastal town through our brand-new twelve-book continuity… You are welcomed to a town where the fishing boats bob up and down in the bay, surfers wait expectantly for the waves, friendly faces line the cobbled streets and romance flutters on the Cornish sea breeze…

We introduce you to Penhally Bay Surgery, where you can meet the team led by caring and commanding Dr Nick Tremayne. Each book will bring you an emotional, tempting romance—from Mediterranean heroes to a sheikh with a guarded heart. There's royal scandal that leads to marriage for a baby's sake, and handsome playboys are tamed by their blushing brides! Top-notch city surgeons win adoring smiles from the community, and little miracle babies will warm your hearts. But that's not all…

With Penhally Bay you get double the reading pleasure… as each book also follows the life of damaged hero Dr Nick Tremayne. His story will pierce your heart—a tale of lost love and the torment of forbidden romance. Dr Nick's unquestionable, unrelenting skill would leave any patient happy in the knowledge that she's in safe hands, and is a testament to the ability and dedication of all the staff at Penhally Bay Surgery. Come in and meet them for yourself…

**Dear Reader**

When my editor phoned to ask if I'd like to take part in an exciting new Medical™ Romance series called *Brides of Penhally Bay*, I said, 'Ummm…who, or what, is Penhally?' The minute she told me about the fictitious Cornish town I was interested. Then, when she told me the names of the other authors who would be taking part, I was hooked. But it was when she told me in what way she'd like me to contribute I knew I would never be able to say no.

There was Tom Cornish, for a start. On the surface this man has it all. Good-looks, a high-powered job as head of operations at the worldwide rescue team of Deltaron, and the complete dedication of his team. But does Tom *really* have it all? And what about Eve? She and Tom haven't seen each other in twenty years, and she's now a dedicated, responsible nurse, a pillar of the community. But she has a secret. A secret which will rock Tom on his heels and change both his and Eve's life for ever.

I confess I grew to love both these characters. They got into my head, and into my heart, and when I finally said goodbye to them it was one of the hardest things I've ever done. They'd become friends. People I'd both laughed with and cried with. People I desperately wanted to help. And one of the joys for me as a writer has been that all the writers who contributed to the series had the same aim. We all wanted to create something really special to commemorate Mills & Boon's one hundredth birthday. I think we succeeded with the *Penhally* series, and I hope you do, too!

Best wishes

*Maggie*

# A BABY FOR EVE

BY
MAGGIE KINGSLEY

MILLS & BOON®
*Pure reading pleasure*™

*This book is dedicated to five extremely talented and generous writing friends. Kate Hardy, Jessica Matthews, Margaret McDonagh, Alison Roberts and Jennifer Taylor. Without their encouragement I can truthfully say this book would never have been finished.*

First published in Great Britain 2008
Harlequin Mills & Boon Limited,
Eton House, 18-24 Paradise Road, Richmond, Surrey TW9 1SR

© Maggie Kingsley 2008

ISBN: 978 0 263 86350 5

Set in Times Roman 10 on 11½ pt
03-1008-54476

Printed and bound in Spain
by Litografia Rosés, S.A., Barcelona

**Maggie Kingsley** says she can't remember a time when she didn't want to be a writer, but she put her dream on hold and decided to 'be sensible' and become a teacher instead. Five years at the chalk face was enough to convince her she wasn't cut out for it, and she 'escaped' to work for a major charity. Unfortunately—or fortunately!—a back injury ended her career, and when she and her family moved to a remote cottage in the north of Scotland it was her family who nagged her into attempting to make her dream a reality. Combining a love of romantic fiction with a knowledge of medicine gleaned from the many professionals in her family, Maggie says she can't now imagine ever being able to have so much fun legally doing anything else!

**Recent titles by the same author:**

# CHAPTER ONE

A WRY smile curved Eve Dwyer's lips as the door of St Mark's Church creaked open then closed again. Somebody was cutting it fine. Very fine. Another five minutes and the wedding ceremony would have begun, and curiously she glanced over her shoulder to see who the latecomer might be only for the smile on her face to freeze.

It was him. His thick black hair might be lightly flecked with grey now, and there were deep lines on his forehead that hadn't been there twenty years ago, but Eve would have recognised the man walking rapidly towards an empty seat near the front of the church anywhere. Tom Cornish was back in Penhally Bay and, if she hadn't been sitting in the middle of a packed pew, surrounded by her colleagues from the village's medical practice, Eve would have taken to her heels and run.

'Good heavens,' Kate Althorp, the village's senior midwife, whispered from Eve's left. 'Is that who I think it is?'

Other people were muttering the same thing, Eve noticed, seeing the number of heads suddenly craning in Tom's direction, the nudges people were giving their neighbours. Not the younger members of the congregation. They wouldn't remember a Dr Tom Cornish but those aged over forty-five certainly did, and not very kindly if the frowns on some faces were anything to go by.

'Is that who?' Lauren Nightingale asked from Eve's right, but Kate didn't have time to answer the physiotherapist.

The organist had launched into the wedding march, which meant the bride had arrived. A bride Tom Cornish wouldn't have known from a cake of soap, Eve thought, gripping her order of service card so tightly that the embossed card bent beneath her fingers. Both Alison Myers and her bridegroom, Jack Tremayne, would have been children when Tom had last been in Penhally Bay so why was he here, and why had he come back when he'd always sworn he never would?

'Doesn't Alison look lovely?' Lauren sighed as the girl walked past them, radiant in a simple long gown of cream satin.

Alison did, but any enjoyment Eve might have felt in the occasion had gone. The flowers in the church, which had smelt so sweet just a few minutes ago, now seemed cloying. The crush of bodies, which had once felt so companionable, now simply felt oppressive, and even the sight of Jack and Alison's small sons, walking solemnly down the aisle behind Alison, failed to give her pleasure.

'Eve, are you OK?'

Kate was gazing curiously at her, and Eve faked a smile.

'I'm fine,' she murmured. 'It's just a bit...crowded.'

The midwife chuckled. 'Penhally loves a wedding. A christening's good, but a wedding is the only thing guaranteed to get the whole village out.'

But not Tom Cornish, Eve thought, stiffening slightly as she saw him half turn in his seat. Tom who had once said marriage was a prison he had no intention of ever inhabiting. Tom who'd said he wanted to be free, to travel, and was damned if he was going to rot away in the village in which he had been born.

'Oh, aren't they sweet?' Lauren exclaimed as Alison's three-year-old son, Sam, and Jack's equally young son, Freddie, held out the red velvet cushions they were carrying so everyone could see the wedding rings sitting on them.

'Yes,' was all Eve could manage as a collective sigh of approval ran round the congregation.

Why was Tom here—*why*? She'd read in a medical magazine a few years back that he'd been appointed head of operations at Deltaron, the world-famous international rescue team, so he should have been somewhere abroad, helping the victims of some disaster, not sitting in the front pew of St Mark's, resurrecting all her old heartache, and anger, and pain.

'Eve, are you *quite* sure you're OK?' Kate whispered, the worry in her eyes rekindling.

'I…I have a bit of a headache, that's all,' Eve lied. 'It's the flowers—the perfume—strong smells always give me a headache.'

Kate looked partially convinced. Not wholly convinced, but at least partially, and Eve gripped her order of service card even tighter.

Pull yourself together, she told herself as the service continued and she found her eyes continually straying away from the young couple standing in front of Reverend Kenner towards Tom. For God's sake, you're forty-two years old, not a girl any more. Tom probably won't even remember you, far less recognise you, so pull yourself together, but she couldn't. No matter how often she told herself she was being stupid, overreacting, all she wanted was to leave. Immediately.

'Eve, you look terrible,' Kate murmured when Jack and Alison had walked back down the aisle as man and wife, and everyone in the congregation began to get to their feet. 'I have some paracetamol in my bag—'

'Air,' Eve muttered. 'I just… I need some fresh air.'

And to get as far away from here as I can before Tom sees me, she added mentally as she hurried to the church door and out into the sunshine. She wasn't tall—just five feet five—so, if she was quick, she could lose herself amongst the congregation, then hurry down Harbour Road and go home. She'd tell everyone at the practice on Monday she'd had a migraine, and her colleagues would understand, she knew they would. All she had to do was keep walking, not look back, and—

'*Eve Dwyer*. By all that's wonderful, it's you, isn't it?'

His voice hadn't changed at all, Eve thought as she came to a halt, moistening lips that had suddenly gone dry. It was as deep and mellow as it had always been, still with that faint trace of Cornish burr, and she wanted to pretend she hadn't heard him, but she couldn't.

'Eve Dwyer,' Tom repeated, shaking his head in clear disbelief as she turned slowly to face him. 'I never expected to run into you within minutes of coming back to Penhally. It's Tom Cornish,' he added a little uncertainly when she stared up at him, completely unable to say a word. 'Don't tell me you've forgotten me?'

How could I? she wanted to reply, but she didn't.

'Of course I remember you, Tom,' she said instead. 'You're…you're looking well.'

He was. Up close, she could see he was heavier now than he had been at twenty-four but on him the extra weight looked good, and the grey in his hair, and the lines on his forehead, gave his face a strength it hadn't possessed before, but it was his eyes that took her breath away.

For years those startlingly green eyes had plagued her dreams, teasing her, laughing at her, and she'd told herself that time and absence had created an unreal image of him, but they were every bit as green as she had remembered, and every bit as potent, and she had to swallow, hard.

'So…'

'So…'

They'd spoken together, and she felt a tingle of heat darken her cheeks.

'I didn't realise you knew Alison and Jack,' she said to fill the silence.

'Who?' He frowned.

'The couple whose wedding you've just been at,' she declared, moving swiftly to one side so the people who were still leaving the church could get past her.

'Never met either of them in my life,' he said.

'Then why come to their wedding?' she asked in confusion.

'I arrived in Penhally just before twelve o'clock, found the place deserted, and when I asked at the shop I was told everybody was probably here.'

Which still didn't explain why he'd come.

'Tom—'

'Tom Cornish.' Kate beamed. 'What in the world brings you back to Penhally? I thought you were still in the States.'

For a second Tom stared blankly at the midwife, clearly trying to place her, then grinned. 'Kate Templar, right?'

'Kate Althorp now, Tom.' She laughed. 'Have been for years.'

And he hadn't answered Kate's question either, Eve thought.

'Are you coming to the reception?' Kate continued, waving to Reverend Kenner as he hurried towards his car. 'It's a buffet at The Smugglers' Inn so there'll be plenty of food, and I'm sure Alison and Jack would be delighted to meet you.'

'And I'm sure Tom has better things to do than go to a reception that will be packed with doctors and nurses who'll only end up talking shop,' Eve said quickly, and saw one of Tom's eyebrows lift.

'I can talk shop,' he said. 'I'm a doctor, too, remember, so I can talk shop with the best of them.'

'Yes, but—'

'Afraid I might embarrass you by smashing up the furniture, getting drunk and insulting all your friends?' he said dryly, and she crimsoned.

'Of course not,' she protested, though, in truth, she wasn't one hundred per cent sure about the insults. 'I just thought…'

She came to a halt. A small hand had slipped into hers. A hand that belonged to a little girl with long blonde hair who was staring up at her eagerly. 'Tassie, sweetheart. Where in the world did you spring from?'

'I've been out here since the wedding started,' the ten-year-old replied. 'Sitting on the wall, listening to the music.'

'Oh, Tassie, love, why didn't you come inside the church?' Eve exclaimed, her gaze taking in the girl's thin and worn T-shirt and her shabby cotton trousers, which weren't nearly warm enough to withstand the cool of the early October day. 'There's quite a breeze blowing in from the harbour—'

'Don't feel the cold,' Tassie interrupted, 'and I'm not really wearing the right sort of clothes for a wedding. Her dress is pretty, isn't it?' she added, gazing wistfully towards the lychgate where Alison and Jack were having their photographs taken.

'Yes, it's very pretty,' Eve murmured, her heart twisting slightly at the envy she could see in the little girl's brown eyes. Eyes which had always seemed too large for her thin face even when she'd been a toddler. 'Tassie, does your mother know you're here?'

'She said I was to get out from under her feet, so I did. She won't be worried.'

Amanda Lovelace probably wouldn't, Eve thought with a sigh, but that wasn't the point.

'Tassie—'

'I was wondering whether I could come to the reception?' the girl interrupted. 'I heard Mrs Althorp say there would be lots of food, so could I come? I won't be any trouble—I promise.'

Eve's heart sank. Normally she couldn't refuse Tassie anything. The child had so few treats in her life, but she didn't want to go to the reception. She didn't want to go anywhere but home.

'Tassie, the reception's not really for children,' she began. 'It's more a grown-up thing.'

'Nonsense!' Kate exclaimed. 'My son Jem will be there and he's only nine. And Alison's son Sam and Jack's son Freddie are both going, and they're only three, so I'm sure Tassie would enjoy it.'

'Perhaps,' Eve declared, 'but I really don't think—'

'Oh, I do, most definitely,' Tom interrupted. 'If Tom Cornish can be given an invitation then I think this half-pint should have one, too.'

'But her mother won't know where she is,' Eve protested, all too aware she was losing this argument, but determined to give it one last try. 'She'll be worried.'

Tom delved into his pocket and produced his mobile phone.

'Not if we use the wonders of modern technology,' he declared. 'Give her a quick call, and then I'll get to take two beautiful women out to lunch.'

Tassie giggled, and Eve sighed inwardly. There was nothing left to say—no argument she could come up with—and when she reluctantly took the phone Kate beamed.

'That's settled, then,' the midwife said as Eve made her call then handed back the phone to Tom. 'Tom, Eve can show you how to get to The Smugglers' Inn if you've forgotten where it is, and...' She stopped in mid-sentence as a dull, metallic thud suddenly split the air followed by the sound of breaking glass. 'What the...?'

'Sounds like someone's just backed into something,' Tom observed.

'And no prizes for guessing who the "someone" is.' Kate groaned as Lauren clambered out of her car, her hand pressed to her mouth.

'Oh, come on, be fair, Kate,' Eve protested. 'The cars are parked really close to one another. Whose car did she hit?'

Kate frowned. 'Don't know. It's a metallic blue Range Rover, not from around here by its number plate, so my guess is it belongs to some flash holidaymaker.'

Tom cleared his throat. 'I'm afraid I'm the flash holiday-maker, so who is the "she" who has just reversed into my car?'

Kate looked uncomfortably at Eve, and Eve bit her lip.

'Lauren. She's our practice physiotherapist, and a really lovely woman, but quite dreadfully accident prone.'

And currently absolutely mortified, Eve thought as Lauren hurried towards them, her cheeks scarlet, her eyes worried.

'I was certain I had enough space to reverse,' she exclaimed, 'absolutely certain, but... Does anyone know who owns the blue Range Rover?'

'Tom does,' Eve replied. 'Tom, this is Lauren Nightingale.'

'Not Florence?' he said, and Eve rolled her eyes.

'Tom, Lauren must have heard that joke about a million times.'

'A million and one now, actually,' Lauren said, 'but that's not the point. I'm so sorry about your car—'

'From the looks of it, your Renault's come off worse,' Tom interrupted, gazing critically at his car, then at Lauren's. 'You've scraped quite a bit of paintwork off your tail, whereas you've only broken my indicator light cover.'

'Which I will pay for,' Lauren insisted, digging into her bag. 'I have my insurance certificate in here—'

'Look, how about I simply send you the bill for the repair, and we don't involve our insurance companies at all?' Tom suggested. 'That way you won't lose your no-claims bonus.'

'Are you sure?' Lauren said uncertainly, and, when Tom nodded, she extracted a notebook and a pen from her bag. 'You'll need my address for the bill. It's Gatehouse Cottage. That's—'

'The cottage at the bottom of the drive that leads to the Manor House.' Tom smiled when the physiotherapist looked at him in surprise. 'I was born in Penhally, lived here for the first twenty-four years of my life, so I know where everything is.'

'Where are you staying so I can contact you?' Lauren asked.

'The Anchor Hotel,' Tom replied, taking the notebook and pen from Lauren, 'but I won't be there long so you'd better have my London address.'

His London address. So he didn't live in the States any more, Eve thought as she watched him scribble in Lauren's notebook, and he wasn't going to be staying in The Anchor for long, but did that mean he was moving back into his old home in Penhally, or what?

'You're staying at The Anchor Hotel?' Kate said before Eve could ask the questions she so desperately wanted the answers to. 'Very posh.'

'You mean, you're amazed they let anyone called Cornish through the door?' Tom said with an edge, and Kate coloured deeply.

'Of course I didn't mean that!' she exclaimed. 'I just meant…'

Her voice trailed away into awkward, embarrassed silence, and Eve came to her rescue.

'Kate, shouldn't you be making tracks for The Smugglers'?' she said. 'Alison and Jack headed off a few minutes ago, and they must be wondering where you are.'

'Oh. Right,' the midwife declared with a grateful smile and, as she and Lauren both headed for their cars, Eve turned to Tom, her expression sad.

'So, it still pushes all your buttons, does it, even after all these years?'

Tom's face tightened.

'Only in Penhally,' he said, then forced a smile as he noticed Tassie gazing up at him in obvious confusion. 'Well, half-pint, what are we waiting for? If we don't get to the reception fast all the best food will have gone.'

'Are we going in your car?' the little girl asked. 'The one that got hit?'

'We can walk,' Eve said hurriedly. 'The Smugglers' isn't far—just up the road.'

'We drive,' Tom insisted. 'If I'm taking two gorgeous women out to lunch then we go in style, even if my car is missing one indicator light cover.'

Walking would be better, Eve thought. Tassie would leap about as she always did, pointing things out to Tom, which would mean she wouldn't have to talk to him, but she could hardly insist on them walking. Tom would wonder why, and if Tom was the same man she had known—and she strongly suspected he was—he would badger and badger her until she told him.

'In style it is, then,' she declared, striding determinedly towards his car before she lost her nerve.

'Can I sit in the front?' Tassie asked, hopping excitedly from one foot to the other, her fine blonde hair flying about her shoulders, and Tom shook his head.

'Surely you know royalty always rides in the back behind the chauffeur?' he replied.

'But I'm not royalty,' the little girl pointed out, and Tom smiled the smile Eve knew could charm the birds off the trees.

'Today you are,' he said, helping Tassie up into the Range Rover. 'So, where to, ma'am?'

'Smugglers' Inn, as quick as you can, driver,' Tassie declared with an imperious air that was completely ruined when she dissolved into a fit of giggles.

'That was kind,' Eve murmured, as she got into the front seat, and Tom slipped into the driver's seat beside her.

'It's only manners to open a door for a lady,' he replied, and Eve shook her head.

'I meant it was kind of you to be so nice to Tassie.'

'She's a nice kid.'

'Not everyone sees that,' Eve observed, then managed a smile when Tom stared at her curiously. 'Do you honestly remember where everything in Penhally is, or do you want directions for The Smugglers'?'

'I haven't forgotten anything about Penhally,' he said abruptly, then grimaced as a slight frown creased Eve's forehead. 'Sorry. An hour back in the place, and already I'm defensive. No, I don't need directions,' he added as he drove out of the car park and turned left. 'The Smugglers' is at the top of Mevagissey Road.'

Odd, she thought as he drove north, that he should remember that. They'd never been to the inn when they'd been younger. It had been too expensive for them when he'd just qualified as a doctor and she'd just finished her nurse's training, and yet he'd remembered where it was. What else did he remember? she wondered, but she didn't want to go down that particular memory lane. It was fraught with too many dangers, too many complications.

'How long have you lived in London?' she said, deliberately changing the conversation. 'I mean, I thought you were still in the States,' she continued as he glanced across at her, 'but you gave Lauren a London address.'

'I haven't lived in the States for the past ten years,' he replied. 'I have a flat in London now, and an apartment in Lausanne overlooking Lake Geneva.'

'Sounds—'

'Posh?' he finished for her dryly, and she shook her head at him.

'Lovely—I was going to say lovely,' she said, and Tom shrugged.

'They're just places I stay in between trips, not proper homes. Homes have people you love in them. Wives, children.'

Don't ask, she thought as she stared out the windscreen at the trees flashing by. Trees that were beginning to lose their leaves under a sky that was as blue as only a Cornish sky could be. She didn't need to know, and it was better if she didn't, but she couldn't help herself.

'You're not married, then?' she said, glancing across at him.

'Nope,' he replied, braking slightly to avoid the rabbit that had dashed out in front of them. 'Never found anyone prepared to put up with the kind of erratic work patterns my job demands. At least, not for any length of time.' His green eyes met hers. 'What about you?'

She shifted her gaze back at the trees.

'No, I'm not married.' She took a deep breath. 'Tom, are you planning on coming back to Penhally to stay, or…?'

'I'm only here until Monday. I have things to do—sort out—then I'll be off again.'

A surge of relief engulfed her. Monday. This was Saturday. She could cope with that. If she should accidentally meet him again tomorrow, she'd be pleasant and friendly, talk about everything and nothing. She'd managed to keep silent for all these years so she could keep quiet for one more day because what good would it do to tell him? Telling him wouldn't change anything, alter anything, make it less painful.

'Eve?'

He was staring curiously at her, and she managed to smile.

'I read in a magazine a while back that you'd been made head of rescue operations at Deltaron,' she said. 'You must be very pleased.'

'Yeah, well, it's certainly a whole different ball game when your desk is the one the buck stops on. What about you?' he asked. 'Still nursing?'

She nodded.

'I actually just started work in Penhally last month,' she said. 'Before that I worked in Truro and Newquay, but Alison—the girl you don't know whose wedding you were just at,' she added, and saw Tom smile, 'is pregnant so I've temporarily taken over her position as practice nurse in the Penhally surgery.'

'Which means if she comes back after her maternity leave, you'll be out of a job,' Tom observed.

'Not for long,' she said briskly. 'There's a big shortage of nurses in the UK so I'll get something else pretty fast.'

'But you'd rather work here, in your home village.'

It was a statement, not a question, and her lips curved wryly.

'Well, you always did say I had no imagination.'

'Did I say that?' He shook his head. 'God, I had a big mouth when I was twenty-four, didn't I?'

'Uh-huh,' she replied, and he laughed. 'Actually, although you don't know Alison or Jack,' she continued, 'you do know Jack's father. It's Nick Tremayne.'

'Nick Tremayne, the doctor?' Tom declared.

'The very same,' Eve answered. 'He's the senior partner in the Penhally surgery now, and my boss.'

'Are you telling me I've just been to the wedding of the *son* of somebody I went to med school with?' Tom groaned. 'God, but now you've made me feel old.'

Eve chuckled. 'Do you remember when we thought anyone older than forty was decrepit?'

'And anyone over fifty might just as well be dead.' He nodded. 'Shows how little we knew, doesn't it?' His eyes met hers again. 'Eve—'

'Are we almost there yet?' Tassie chipped in from the back of the car. 'I'm *starving.*'

'In other words, quit with the talking,' Tom said ruefully, 'and drive faster.'

'Something like that.' The little girl giggled and, as Tom grinned across at Eve, and her own lips curved in response, her heart contracted.

No, she told herself. *No.* The past is past, nobody can ever go back, and if you allow yourself to be sucked back into his world he'll only hurt you again, and this time you might not survive.

'What's wrong?' Tom asked, his green eyes suddenly puzzled, and Eve shook her head.

'Just hungry, like Tassie.'

'Eve—'

'We're here!' Tassie interrupted with a shriek as the grey-stoned façade of The Smugglers' Inn suddenly came into view. 'And look at all the cars. I hope there's room inside for us.'

And I hope it's standing room only, Eve thought, so I can hide myself in the crush, but Tom must have read her mind because as she got out of the car he took her arm firmly in his.

'Now we eat, and socialise, right?' he declared.

'You go ahead,' Eve replied. 'I just need…'

She waved vaguely in the direction of the door leading to the ladies' cloakroom, but it didn't do her any good.

'We'll wait for you, won't we, Tassie?' Tom said, and Tassie beamed, leaving Eve with nothing to do but obediently disappear into the ladies' cloakroom.

At least it was empty, she thought with relief as she walked in. Company was the last thing she wanted right now, and quickly she washed her hands then pulled her hairbrush out of her handbag. Lord, but she looked awful. White face, panic-stricken brown eyes, her shoulder-length brown hair slightly windswept, and…

Forty-two, she thought bleakly as she gazed at her reflection in the mirror over the sink. I look forty-two. OK, so that wasn't old, but nothing could alter the fact that she was heavier than she'd been at twenty-two, that there were faint lines at the corner of her eyes, and her hair wouldn't be brown if Vicki at the hairdresser's didn't tint it every six weeks.

Impatiently, she dragged her hairbrush through her hair. What did it matter if she didn't look twenty-two any more?

Because I would like to have looked as I did when he last saw me, her heart sighed as her eyes met those in the mirror. Because it would have shown him what he lost when he walked away from me, and it was stupid to feel that way. Stupid.

'Feeling any better now?'

Eve whirled round to see Kate Althorp standing behind her, and forced a smile.

'Much,' she lied, and Kate shot her a shrewd glance as she ran some water into a sink and began washing her hands.

'It must have been quite a shock to see Tom again.'

'A surprise,' Eve said firmly. 'It was a surprise, that's all, seeing him back in Penhally.'

'Yes, but you and he were quite close before he went to the States, weren't you?'

*Close.* What an, oh, so very British, euphemistic way of saying 'lovers', Eve thought wryly, and of course Kate would remember she and Tom had spent that summer together. Kate was in her forties, too, and nothing stayed a secret for long in Penhally unless you really worked at it, and Tom hadn't given a damn about what people thought.

'Kate, I was twenty-two, he was twenty-four,' Eve declared, injecting as much careless indifference into her voice as she could. 'We shared a short summer romance, that's all.'

'Which wouldn't make it any the less painful when it ended,' Kate Althorp said gently.

The midwife saw too much—way too much—and Eve picked up her hairbrush again.

'Water under the bridge years ago,' she said. 'We've both gone our separate ways since then, led very different lives.'

Or at least Tom had, Eve thought as Kate looked for a moment as though she'd like to say something, then dried her hands on a paper towel and left the cloakroom. Tom had gone off to the States, full of determination to succeed, and he had, whereas she…

She squeezed her eyes shut. He was not going to do this to her. She had spent all these years rebuilding her life into something to be proud of, something that mattered, and she was not going to let his presence tear it all down, make it seem worthless.

'Enough, Eve,' she said as she opened her eyes and gazed at her reflection again. 'The past is past. Don't resurrect it.'

Except it wasn't that easy, she realised as she walked out of the cloakroom, and found Tom and Tassie waiting for her, grinning like a pair of conspirators.

'Tassie was convinced you'd slipped down the toilet,' Tom declared. 'I told her we'd give you another five minutes, then I'd go over the top in my capacity as head of rescue operations at Deltaron.'

'Promises, promises,' Eve said lightly, and Tom's grin widened.

'You think I wouldn't—or couldn't?' he replied.

'I think we should eat,' she said firmly, refusing to be drawn, but he knew what she was doing.

She could see it in the glint in his eyes. The familiar half daring, half challenging glint which had appeared in the past whenever he'd been about to do, or say, something completely outrageous, and a faint unease stirred in her. An unease which must have shown on her face because he smiled.

'I'm a mature man now, Eve,' he declared. 'No fights, no arguments, I promise.'

And he was as good as his word.

For the next hour Tom charmed his way round the crowded room as only he could when he wanted to. Of course it helped that most of the people at the reception were newcomers to the village, but even when some of the older villagers cut him dead he didn't rise to the bait. He simply moved away with a wry smile to gently reassure Lauren about his car, then make Chloe Mackinnon, the village's other midwife, laugh as her fiancé, Dr Fawkner, stood by, watching protectively.

'He's changed, hasn't he?' Kate observed, nodding towards Tom who was now engaged in an animated discussion about fund-holding practices with Dr Lovak.

'Tom always could string more than two words together, you know,' Eve said more caustically than she'd intended, and Kate's eyebrows rose.

'I never thought he couldn't,' the midwife replied. 'Just as you also know I never thought he got a fair deal in Penhally.'

'Still won't, judging by the reaction of some people,' Eve said, nodding across to a small group of villagers who were throwing deep frowns in Tom's direction.

'People have long memories and old prejudices. I'm not saying they're right,' Kate continued as Eve opened her mouth to interrupt. 'In fact, the longer I've lived, the less inclined I've become to judge anyone, but don't forget Tom has friends here, too, as well as detractors.'

Name one, apart from yourself, Eve was tempted to say, but she didn't.

'I must get Tassie home,' she said instead. 'She's beginning to look tired.'

Tom clearly wasn't because the minute Eve began to make her way through the throng he was instantly at her side.

'Trying to run out on me, are you?' he said, and she shook her head at him.

'It's time I took Tassie home,' she replied, sidestepping quickly as Freddie and Sam dashed past them, slipping and sliding on the polished wooden floor, whooping at the top of their lungs.

'Regular little bundles of fun, aren't they?' Tom said with amusement as the youngsters scampered off.

'You used to hate kids,' Eve reminded him. 'Said they should all be kept indoors by their parents until they were teenagers.'

'Yeah, well...' Tom glanced back at the two boys. 'Do you ever find yourself wishing you'd had children?'

Eve stared fixedly at the wedding cake sitting on the table by the window.

'No point in wishing, Tom,' she said. 'It's better to deal with the here and now.'

'I guess so,' he said, then smiled and waved to Tassie. 'But I still think I'd like to have kids.'

'And I think it's way past time Tassie went home,' Eve said through a throat so tight it hurt.

'Eve—'

'Well, well, well. If it isn't Tom Cornish. And what brings Penhally's local-boy-made-good back to Cornwall?'

Eve glanced over her shoulder to see Nick Tremayne standing behind them, and smiled.

'Tom,' she began, 'this is—'

'Nick Tremayne.' Tom grinned. 'No need for an introduction, Eve. I would have recognised this old reprobate anywhere. Good to see you again, Nick, and still doctoring, I hear.'

'And you're still globetrotting with Deltaron if all I've read about you is true,' Nick replied with no smile at all.

'You've been following my career?' Tom said lightly, but Eve could see a slightly puzzled look in his eyes. 'I'm flattered.'

'Oh, even in a sleepy little backwater like Penhally, we have the internet and satellite television now,' Nick replied, 'which means I'm all too aware of your exploits.'

'Tom is just back for a short visit,' Eve said, glancing from Tom to Nick, then back again uncertainly. Lord, but the animosity emanating from Nick was so patent it could have flash-frozen fish. 'He's leaving on Monday.'

'Back to singlehandedly, heroically saving the world, I presume?' Nick declared, and what little smile there had been left on Tom's face disappeared completely.

'If you want heroes, Nick, then it's the people who live in the countries my team and I go into to help who deserve that title,' he said tersely. 'They're the ones who have to tackle the long-term effects of any disaster.'

'I couldn't agree more,' Nick observed, 'but they don't get

the credit, do they? Because they get left with the boring, tedious stuff, like rebuilding their country, while you swan off on yet another photo opportunity.'

'Now, just a minute,' Tom began, his face darkening, and Eve caught hold of his sleeve quickly.

'Tom, we really *do* have to get Tassie home,' she said. 'She's very tired, and I told Amanda we'd make sure she wouldn't be too late back.'

For a moment she didn't think he was going to come with her. He certainly didn't look as though he wanted to as he glared at Nick, and Nick glared back, then he nodded reluctantly.

'Right,' he said, then added, 'See you around, Nick,' before he strode out of the room, leaving Eve and Tassie with nothing to do but hurry after him.

'I thought you said you and Nick Tremayne were friends?' Eve protested when she caught up with him in the car park.

'I thought we were, too,' Tom replied, 'but I've clearly done something to rattle his cage. Any idea what?'

'None at all,' Eve said. 'He can certainly be a bit brusque at times, but he's not normally so…so…'

'In your face?' Tom shook his head as he helped Tassie clamber into his Range Rover. 'Kate Althorp sure had a lucky escape.'

'From what?' Eve asked in confusion.

'From marrying him. Don't you remember how close Kate and Nick were at school?' he continued as Eve looked at him in surprise. 'Everyone was certain they'd get married.'

'Well, they didn't,' Eve replied. 'Kate married James Althorp.'

'So I gathered.' Tom frowned as he switched on his ignition. 'Which I have to say I find surprising. Don't get me wrong,' he added. 'James was a nice enough bloke, but I'd have thought he was a bit too laid back for Kate, which only goes to show you never can tell. Nick married that girl he met at med school, didn't he? Anne…Isabel…'

'Annabel.'

'Yeah, that was her name. Nice girl, she was, too, as I recall.'

'She died nearly three years ago now,' Eve replied. 'Her appendix ruptured and because she'd taken aspirin she bled out and there was nothing anyone could do.'

'I'm sorry about that,' Tom declared, 'but I still reckon Kate had a lucky escape.'

But Nick isn't normally like that, Eve thought with a frown, as Tom drove them down the winding road back into the village. The senior partner could certainly be sharp and cutting if he felt people weren't pulling their weight, but she'd never seen him verbally attack somebody for no reason, and yet that was exactly what he'd done this afternoon.

'Where does Tassie live?' Tom asked as they drove down Harbour Road.

'Just off Morwenna Road, but if you drop us at the post office we can walk from there,' Eve replied.

'But that will still leave you quite a distance to walk,' Tom protested.

'All to the good,' Eve said calmly. 'I need some exercise after what I've eaten.'

'But—'

'Drop us at the post office, Tom.'

He sighed but, after he'd crossed the Harbour Bridge, he obediently pulled up at the post office.

'Thanks for the ride, mister,' Tassie said when she and Eve got out of his car, and he smiled and ruffled her hair.

'Could you make yourself scarce for a couple of minutes, half-pint?' he said. 'I need to talk to Eve.'

'Tom, Tassie really does have to go home,' Eve began as the girl obediently skipped down the road for a few yards, then waited. 'The wind's getting up, and she's not dressed for the weather—'

'I was wondering whether you'd like to come out with me

tomorrow?' he interrupted. 'We could have lunch, and you could show me the sights of Penhally.'

'Tom, you were born here, you know what the sights are,' she protested.

'There's bound to have been some changes—new developments—since I was last here,' he argued back, 'and I thought—perhaps for old times' sake?'

She didn't want to do anything for old times' sake. Two postcards, that's all he'd sent her after he'd left for America. One from New York, saying he was homesick and lonely, and another one from California six months later, saying he'd applied for a job with Deltaron. After that, there'd been nothing. Not a card, or a letter, or a phone call, for the past twenty years during which she'd got on with her life, and if it hadn't been the life she'd planned, dreamed of, it had been a satisfying life, and now he was back, and she didn't want him to be back.

'I'm sorry,' she said firmly. 'I have things to do tomorrow.' '*Please.*'

If he had been smiling at her with that old gotta-love-me smile she would never have wavered, but he wasn't smiling. In fact, he looked uncharacteristically unsure, uncertain, and Tom Cornish had never been unsure of anything in his life.

'I can't do lunch,' she said hesitantly. *Won't, more like.* 'As I said, I have things to do tomorrow.'

'Half a day is better than none,' he said. 'Do you still live in Polkerris Road with your parents? I'll pick you up at two o'clock—'

'Three o'clock,' she interrupted. 'And I'll meet you outside your hotel.'

He looked disappointed, then he nodded.

'OK, three o'clock it is,' he said, then to her surprise he added quickly, 'You will come, won't you?'

The uncertainty was back in his eyes, big time, and a slight frown creased her forehead.

'I said I'd come,' she pointed out, 'and I will.'

Though God knows why, she thought as she joined Tassie and the two of them began walking down the road together.

'He's nice,' Tassie observed, hopping from one paving stone to the next in some sort of elaborate game only she understood.

'Tom can be very nice when he wants to be,' Eve replied noncommittally.

'He told me you and he were best friends when you were younger,' Tassie continued with her usual directness, and Eve manufactured a smile.

'It was a long time ago, Tassie.'

'He still likes you. I can tell. In fact,' the girl added, 'I bet if we turn round right now he'll be watching you from outside the post office.'

'Tassie,' Eve began in consternation, but the girl had already stopped and was looking over her shoulder.

'Told you so,' Tassie said.

'He's watching us?' Eve said faintly.

'See for yourself if you don't believe me,' Tassie declared, and Eve shook her head, feeling her cheeks prickle with heat.

'I've got to get you home.'

'Chicken.' Tassie laughed.

Self-preservation, more like, Eve thought, walking on determinedly. I don't owe him anything, not after all these years.

*But you've still agreed to meet him tomorrow afternoon, haven't you?* a little voice mocked at the back of her mind, and she groaned inwardly.

She must have been out of her mind.

# CHAPTER TWO

IT WAS strange, Tom thought as he leant back against the grey-stoned wall of the Anchor Hotel and breathed in deeply. He'd been all around the world in the course of his work, and yet no air had ever smelt quite the same as the air did in Penhally Bay.

And nobody had ever looked quite like Eve Dwyer, he decided when he heard the faint sound of footsteps in the distance, and turned to see her walking down Fisherman's Row towards him wearing a cherry-red sweater and a russet-coloured skirt, her brown hair gleaming in the early October sunshine.

Lord, but she'd scarcely changed at all. She still had the same cloud of brown hair, the same long, curly eyelashes, and even the same two dimples which peeked out when she smiled. Perhaps she was slightly curvier now than she had been when at twenty-two, but it suited her. It suited her a lot, he decided as his gaze swept over her appreciatively.

'Am I late?' she said, her brown eyes apologetic when she drew level with him.

He shook his head, and breathed in deeply again.

'You know, I think I would recognise Penhally air even if I was blindfolded.'

'You mean the pong of old seaweed and fish?' she said, her eyes dancing.

'I meant the tang of the sea, as you very well know,' he said severely, then his lips curved. 'And there was me thinking you'd still be a romantic.'

The light in her eyes disappeared, and a shadow replaced it.

'Gave up on romance a long time ago, Tom. So…' She spread her hands wide. 'Where do you want to start?'

'Start?' He echoed, still puzzling over what she'd said about giving up on romance.

'You said you wanted a tour of Penhally,' she reminded him. 'So, do you want to go north towards the lighthouse first, or down to the lifeboat station?'

'The lighthouse, I think,' he said. 'You always used to go there when you wanted to think, didn't you?'

She shot him a surprised glance.

'What an odd thing to remember,' she said.

'Oh, my mind's a regular ragbag of odd bits of information,' he replied lightly as she crossed the Harbour Bridge back into Fisherman's Row and he fell into step beside her.

'Of course, not many fishermen live in Fisherman's Row any more,' she declared. 'In fact, there aren't many fishermen left in Penhally full stop. Too few fish to catch nowadays, and too many quotas, to make it a viable way of life.' She waved to a dark-haired young woman who had come out of one of the cottages to scoop up a ginger cat. 'That's Chloe MacKinnon. You met her yesterday at Alison and Jack's reception.'

'Midwife like Kate, yes?' Tom frowned. 'Works in the village practice, and is currently engaged to, and living with, Oliver Fawkner?'

'That's the one,' Eve said as the woman waved back and disappeared into her house. 'You met Oliver at the reception, too.'

'I remember.' Tom nodded, then chuckled. 'You know, if one of the local midwives and a practice doctor had been living together when I was last in Penhally, they'd have been tarred and feathered then run out of town.'

'Times change even in Penhally, at least for some things,' she murmured, and before he could say anything she pointed across the harbour to where a pretty cottage sat high on the hill. 'That's where Kate lives. Her house must have one of the best views in Penhally.'

'Right,' he said, shooting her a puzzled glance.

'Dr Lovak used to live in Fisherman's Row,' Eve continued as they walked past the library and into Harbour Road, 'but he and his wife, Melinda, moved out into the country in the summer. I guess with a baby coming they wanted more space.'

Tom was sure they did, but talking about where the members of the village practice lived was not exactly what he'd had in mind when he'd asked Eve to meet him today, and if she was going to spend the whole afternoon pointing out the homes of her colleagues it was going to be a very long afternoon indeed.

'Eve—'

'I'm sorry,' she broke in, turning to face him, her expression contrite. 'I know I'm babbling a load of boring drivel, but the thing is…' She lifted her shoulders helplessly. 'We don't know each other any more, and I don't know what to say, or talk to you about. I know we were…close…in the past, but—'

'Us meeting again is fast turning into your worst date ever,' he finished for her, and she coloured.

'Maybe not quite that bad, but we're practically strangers now, Tom, so why did you ask to see me again—what was the point?'

Good question, he thought, but how could he tell her that part of him had hoped to find her happily married so he could finally squash the dream that had haunted him for years—that he could somehow go back, change things—while the other part had hoped she was still single so he might be given another chance at happiness.

She would say he wasn't making any sense, and maybe he wasn't. Maybe nobody could—or should—ever try to go back.

'Look, I won't take offence if you just want to give this up, and go back to your hotel,' Eve continued.

If her eyes hadn't met his when she'd spoken he might have been tempted to accept her suggestion, but, lord, she really was as lovely as he'd remembered, and how could he have forgotten her eyes weren't simply brown, but had tiny flecks of green in them? Because he'd forced himself to forget, he thought with a sigh, spent so many years trying not to remember, until a year ago, when...

Don't go there, his mind warned. It's better not to go there. 'Tom?'

She looked awkward and uncomfortable, and he forced a smile.

'Of course I don't want to go back to the hotel,' he said. 'Leastways, not until you've pointed out Nick's house and I've thrown a brick through his window.'

She gave a small choke of laughter. 'I thought you said you were a mature man now?'

'OK, I'll see if I can capture some greenfly and let them loose on his roses instead,' he said, and when she laughed out loud he linked his arm with hers, and began walking again. 'Eve, I know it's been a long time since we last met,' he continued, 'but it simply means we've a lot of catching up to do. And speaking of catching up,' he added when she said nothing, 'are you *quite* sure you don't know why Nick appears to consider me dog meat?'

'I thought you might know the answer to that,' she observed, and he shook his head.

'I knew him at school, and met him a couple of times when I went to med school, but he was a few years older than me, and his friends tended to be the more studious type, whereas mine...' He grinned down at her. 'Tended to be a little rowdier.'

'I bet they were,' Eve said dryly.

'How many kids does Nick have?' Tom asked, and Eve smiled as they reached the end of Harbour Road and turned towards the lighthouse.

'He and Annabel had three of a family. Lucy and Jack, who are twins, and Edward. They're all doctors.'

Tom pulled a face. 'All of them! I don't think I'd want any kids of mine becoming medics, would you?'

. He'd said the wrong thing. He didn't know why, or how, but her face had suddenly closed up completely, and he longed to hug her, or say something totally outrageous to bring the smile back onto her face, but no words occurred to him, and as for hugging her... In the past he wouldn't have thought twice, but even thinking about doing it now made him feel ridiculously awkward, as though it would be too forward which was crazy when he remembered what they'd once meant to one another.

'Odd time of day for a church service,' he said, deliberately changing the subject as they passed the church and the sound of enthusiastic singing drifted out.

'It's not a service,' Eve replied. 'Reverend Kenner runs a club for the village youngsters on Sunday afternoons. Daniel's a nice man. A good one, too.'

'Single, is he?' Tom said, feeling a spurt of something that crazily felt almost like jealousy.

'Daniel's a widower like Nick, with a seventeen-year-old daughter.'

And she didn't look any happier, Tom thought as they walked on to the lighthouse. In fact, she looked even more strained and, in desperation, he pointed out to sea to where the wreck of the seventeenth century Spanish galleon, the *Corazón del Oro*, had lain for the past four hundred years.

'Remember when we wished we could dive down there, find loads of gold coins, and make our fortune?'

'Except neither of us could swim, so it was a bit of a non-starter,' she replied. 'Still can't swim, which is a dreadful admission for somebody who lives by the sea. What about you?'

'I had to learn for my work so they sent me on a course and, believe me, being in a class of five-year-olds when you're twenty-four, and five feet ten inches tall, doesn't do a lot for your ego.'

Her lips twitched. 'You're making that up.'

'Scout's honour,' he protested, and she laughed.

'Tom, you were thrown out of the Scouts for disruptive behaviour when you were thirteen.'

'OK, so maybe I was,' he said, relieved to see her smile again, 'but I honestly was stuck in a kids' class. My boss reckoned it would concentrate my mind wonderfully, and it did. I always wondered why your dad didn't teach you to swim, what with him being a sailor.'

'He was too busy trying to make a living. My mum wanted me to learn, but you had to pay for lessons, and…' She shrugged. 'Money was always tight when I was a kid.'

'Are they still alive—your mum and dad?' he asked, as they turned and began walking back from the lighthouse.

She shook her head.

'My dad died of cancer fifteen years ago. Never would give up his cigarettes, though Mum nagged him like crazy about it. My mum died of a heart attack five years ago.'

'I'm sorry,' he said gently. 'I know they were apoplectic that summer when we started dating, but I liked them.'

'So did I,' she murmured, and Tom swore under his breath.

Hell, but she had that look on her face again. That bleak, almost haunted look as though he had conjured up memories that would have been better left buried.

'Look, why don't we go down to the beach?' he said quickly. 'Have a walk along the sand.'

'I'm not really dressed for it, Tom,' she replied, pointing down at her shoes. 'My heels will get stuck.'

'Then take your shoes off,' he said. 'Take off your stockings, too, and you can paddle if you want.'

'Tom, it's October,' she said. 'It's too cold to paddle.'

'Rubbish,' he said, steering her firmly towards the steps that led down to the beach. 'It's a gorgeous day.'

It was, too, Eve thought as she stared up at the sky. Seagulls were wheeling and diving overhead, their white feathers standing out in sharp contrast to the clear blue sky, and there was a deceptive warmth in the air despite the fact that it was October. Soon it would change. Soon it would be winter and the green-blue sea would become grey and stormy, sending breakers crashing onto the white sand, and only the very toughest would walk along the shore, but today there was enough heat in the day to make it pleasant.

'If you hurry up,' Tom continued as he sat down on the top step, and began pulling off his shoes and socks, and rolling up his trousers, 'we'll have the beach to ourselves—just the way you used to like it.'

How had he remembered that? she thought with surprise, and he'd also remembered she used to sit at the foot of the lighthouse when she wanted to think. They were such little things—such inconsequential things— and yet he'd remembered, and the water did look tempting, so very tempting, but she could just imagine what the gossipmongers would say if somebody saw her.

*Eve Dwyer went paddling with that Tom Cornish yesterday.* Paddling, *and with that Tom Cornish.*

'Tom, maybe we should just go back into the village,' she began, and his green eyes danced as he looked up at her.

'Eve, I'm not suggesting we go skinny-dipping. Though I'm game if you are.'

Her lips curved in spite of herself.

'In your dreams,' she said.

'Chicken.'

He was the second person to have called her that in twenty-four hours, and she discovered she didn't like it. She didn't like it one bit. OK, so skinny-dipping was completely out of the question but, hell's bells, even in Penhally she could surely paddle if she wanted to, and she discovered she wanted to.

'OK, move over,' she said, and he slid across the step so she could sit down beside him.

'So, are we paddling, or skinny-dipping?' he said, and, when she gave him a hard stare, his eyes glinted. 'Pity. I was kind of looking forward to shocking the good people of Penhally.'

'I bet you were,' she said dryly as she unbuckled the straps of her shoes and slipped them off. 'Right. Turn your back while I take off my stockings,' she added, and when his mouth fell open, she said, 'I'm not having you staring at my thighs, and making snarky comments about cellulite, so turn your back.'

'I don't even know what cellulite is,' he protested, but he did as she asked, and when she eventually stuffed her tights into her skirt pocket and stood up, he said, 'You're an idiot—you know that, don't you?'

'Probably,' she agreed, picking up her shoes by their straps, and walking down the steps. 'So, are we walking or not?'

He shook his head at her as he followed her down the steps.

'You didn't used to be so shy,' he observed, and a stain of colour spread across her cheeks.

He was laughing at her, she knew he was, remembering all the times he'd seen her completely naked, and she bit her lip, waiting for him to point that out, but he didn't.

'I don't think I'll ever forget you dancing and singing on this beach,' he said instead, completely surprising her. 'It was the height of summer—the place was packed with tourists, and families from the village—and suddenly you began singing that Whitney Houston song at the top of your lungs.'

'"I wanna to dance with somebody"!' she exclaimed with a choke of laughter. 'I'd forgotten all about that. I got into such a row with my mother after Audrey Baxter told her I'd made a public spectacle of myself.'

'Audrey Baxter would say that,' he replied with feeling as they began walking along the beach.

'And you told me I had no taste,' she reminded him. 'That if I wanted to sing, then I should have sung one of Bruce Springsteen's songs because he was the only singer worth listening to.'

'Still is,' he insisted, and when she rolled her eyes he laughed, and said, 'Do you still have that dress?'

'What dress?' she said in confusion.

'The red dress you wore that day. It had a big wide skirt, and puffy sleeves, and when I first went to the States I couldn't turn on the radio without hearing Chris de Burgh singing "The Lady in Red", and every time I heard it I thought of you, singing on this beach.'

'Did you?' she said faintly, and he nodded.

'You wouldn't believe how homesick I got whenever they played that song.'

But not homesick enough to write to me, or phone me, she thought, but she didn't say that.

'I'm afraid I threw the dress out years ago,' she said instead.

'Pity,' he murmured, picking up a pebble and sending it skimming across the water in front of them. 'I always liked that dress, and the little red boots you used to wear.'

'My *pixie boots*!' she exclaimed. 'I'd forgotten all about them, too. I *loved* those boots. Couldn't wear them now, of course.'

'Yes, you could. You've still got great legs. Great figure, too,' he added.

'Not that good,' she said, feeling the wash of colour on her cheeks return as his gaze swept over her. 'Years ago I could eat whatever I wanted and never put on a kilo. Now I just have to look at a cream cake, and, pouf, on goes the weight.'

He grinned. 'Well, you're looking good from where I'm standing.'

So was he, she thought. With the sun on his face, and the

wind ruffling his hair, he looked exactly like the town bad boy he'd been all those years ago, whereas she…

What had she been back then?

Naïve, yes. Trusting, most definitely, but mostly so full of dreams, and hopes, and plans. Tom had been the same, but her dreams hadn't been the same as his. He'd wanted to get as far away from Penhally as he could, to live a life of adventure and excitement, and she… She'd simply wanted him.

'Let's have some fun,' he'd said when he'd come back to Penhally as a fully qualified doctor that summer, and she'd been so happy because he'd finally asked her out that she'd chosen not to believe him when he'd told her he would be heading for the States at the end of September.

He'll change his mind, she'd told herself, and for four wonderful, glorious months they'd walked, and talked—lord, how they'd talked—and they'd made love. She'd been a virgin when they'd first started going out and he'd teased her about it, said a woman could have just as much fun as a man without fear of the consequences, and she'd gone on the Pill to be safe, and then after four far too short months he had left.

'What are you thinking about?'

She looked up to see him gazing at her quizzically, and managed a smile.

'I was just wondering where the last twenty years had gone,' she said. 'Sometimes it seems like a lifetime, doesn't it, and sometimes just a few months.'

'And I can't believe you're still single,' he observed. 'The men in Penhally must be either blind, or stupid, or both.'

'I almost got married once,' she replied, kicking the sand in front of her so it sprayed out as they walked, 'but…'

'It didn't feel right?'

'Something like that. What about you?' she asked. 'Were you never tempted to take the plunge?'

'I've had a couple of semi-serious relationships, but…' He

shrugged. 'My work makes it difficult because I never know where I'm going to be from one day to the next.'

'Maybe you're just not the marrying kind,' she said. 'Some people aren't.'

He stared out to sea, then back at her, and to her surprise he looked suddenly wistful, almost sad.

'And maybe I simply got my priorities all wrong.'

His eyes were fixed on hers, refusing to allow her to look away, and her heart gave an uncomfortable thump. This conversation was getting too personal, way too personal, and she had to change it. Now.

'Last one to reach the end of the beach is a wimp,' she said, and, before he could reply, she was off and running, her bare feet flying over the sand, her skirt billowing above her knees, her shoes swinging from her hand.

From behind her she heard him shout a spluttered protest, but she didn't stop. She just kept on running and when she heard his footsteps begin to thud behind her she suddenly, and inexplicably, began to laugh.

To laugh like the girl she'd once been. The carefree young girl who had once sung on a beach, feeling nothing but the joy of being alive, and she knew she probably looked like a demented lunatic, but she didn't care. For this moment—for just this one moment—with her hair streaming in the breeze, and the taste of the sun and the sea on her lips, she felt like that girl again, and it was wonderful.

'You *cheated*!' he exclaimed when he caught up with her, and grasped her by the waist, spinning her round so fast she had to catch hold of his shirt to prevent herself from toppling over.

'Sore loser,' she threw back at him, laughing breathlessly as she pushed her hair away from her face. 'You've been spending far too much time behind a desk.'

'Too much time...?' His eyes narrowed. 'I'll make you pay for that remark, Eve Dwyer.'

'Oh, no, you won't,' she said, turning to run again, and he made a grab for her, and she jumped back to escape him, only to let out a yell as she ended up ankle deep in the sea. 'Oh, my God, it's *freezing*.'

'Serves you right.' Tom laughed but, when she scooped up some water and threw it at him, he splashed into the water after her. 'Play rough, would you? OK, you deserve a complete ducking for that.'

'You wouldn't,' she cried, trying to evade him, but he caught her round the waist again and swept her up into his arms.

'You think?' he said, deliberately lowering her towards the water, and she shrieked and threw her arms round his neck.

'Tom, no!'

He grinned. 'OK, if you don't want to be ducked, you'll need to pay a forfeit, and I think you know what that forfeit is, don't you?'

A kiss. The forfeit had always been a kiss when they'd dated and, as Eve stared up into his, oh, so familiar face, she realised with a stab of pain that even after all that had happened, even after all the heartache and desolation, she wanted to kiss him, and the thought appalled her.

'Tom, let me go,' she said, but he didn't hear the strain in her voice.

'Nope, not a chance,' he said. 'The forfeit, or the sea. Your choice.'

'Tom, *please*.'

'Make a decision—make a decision,' he insisted as he whirled her round in his arms, but she didn't have to.

She had suddenly seen what he hadn't, and she tugged desperately on his sleeve.

'Tom, we have company.'

'Company?' he repeated, then swore under his breath as he followed her gaze. 'Oh, wonderful. Bloody wonderful. Is that who I think it is?'

'I'm afraid so,' Eve said, through gritted teeth, and when Tom quickly put her down she splashed out of the sea, feeling completely ridiculous and stupid, as Audrey Baxter walked towards them.

'Tom Cornish,' Audrey declared the minute she drew level with them, her faded brown eyes alive with curiosity and speculation. 'My heavens, but I never thought to see you in Penhally again.'

'Us bad pennies have a nasty habit of turning up again, don't we, Mrs Baxter?' he replied dryly.

'Oh, I wouldn't call you a bad penny, Tom,' Audrey declared. 'You were a little wild, to be sure—'

'I think the words you used to shout after me when I was a teenager were, "You're heading straight to hell in a handcart, Tom Cornish".'

Audrey patted her steel-grey curls and shook her head at him reprovingly.

'That was a long time ago, Tom.' She shifted her gaze to Eve, making her all too aware that her hair must be sticking out all over the place, and the hem of her skirt was wet. 'I see you and Nurse Dwyer are getting reacquainted.'

Tom moved up the beach a step. 'We are, but now I'm afraid we have to be going.'

'I thought you might have come back to Penhally two years ago, Tom, when your father died,' Audrey continued. 'I know you didn't always get on—'

'And I think your dog's looking for you,' Tom interrupted, pointing to the brindle and white greyhound which was splashing in the water further up the beach.

'Looking for crabs, more like,' Audrey replied. 'He loves them.'

'Indeed,' Tom declared, 'and now if you'll excuse us…'

But Audrey wasn't about to let him leave so easily.

'I hear your father left you his house in Trelissa Road?' she called after him, and Tom turned slowly to face her, his expression tight.

'What a very knowledgeable little community Penhally is,' he said, the sarcasm in his voice so plain that even Audrey couldn't miss it, and Eve grabbed his hand quickly, not caring that Audrey's eyes followed her action.

'Tom, we really do have to be going,' she insisted, and determinedly she urged him back up the beach, but it wasn't over as far as he was concerned.

'Nothing changes, does it?' he spat out when they reached the steps leading off the beach, and he glanced over his shoulder to see Audrey was watching them. 'Twenty damn years, and nothing changes. I could be the Prime Minister of Britain, and in Penhally I'd still be Tom Cornish, that drunkard, Frank Cornish's, son who no decent family ever wanted their daughter dating.'

'Tom—'

'If you're going to say Audrey meant no harm, you can save your breath,' he interrupted, sitting down on the step and beginning to drag on his socks, heedless of the fact that his feet were still covered in sand. 'And if you were going to ask me why I didn't come back for my father's funeral, you can save your breath on that one, too.'

'I know why you didn't come back, Tom,' she said gently, 'and Audrey… There's no question she can be an interfering busybody, but your father's dead and gone. Don't let him keep hurting you.'

'He left me his house, Eve,' he said furiously. 'After years of battering me from pillar to post until I was big enough to hit him back and make it count, he had the gall to leave me his house.'

'Maybe…' She shrugged helplessly. 'Maybe he was trying to make amends, at the end?'

'If I believed that for one second,' he retorted, 'I'd go round and torch the bloody place myself. No guilt gift can ever make up for the fact he hated me from the day I was born. Time and time again, he'd tell me of all the things he could have done—would have done—if my mother hadn't become pregnant, and her family hadn't forced him into marrying her, and when she died he hated me even more.'

'I know,' she said, sitting down beside him, aching at the pain she saw in his face, feeling a different kind of pain in herself, but he rounded on her furiously.

'No, you don't. You have *no* idea of what it's like to live with a man whose dreams you've shattered. No idea to feel, even as a seven-year-old child, that it would have been better if you'd never been born.'

She opened her mouth, then closed it again.

'I'm sorry,' she murmured. 'You're right. I don't know.'

Silently she brushed the sand from her feet, then pushed her feet into her shoes, but when she made to stand up he put out his hand to stop her.

'You've forgotten your stockings.'

'Doesn't matter,' she replied, and, for a second he said nothing, then he thrust his fingers through his hair, and she saw his hands were shaking.

'I'm sorry,' he said, his voice so strained it almost broke. 'So sorry for yelling at you.'

'It's all right,' she said.

'It's not,' he declared. 'I shouldn't have taken it out on you, and I'm sorry, too, that Audrey saw you in my arms. I know what this place is like—the gossip, the innuendo…'

'It's *all right*, Tom,' she insisted, and saw a small smile creep onto his lips.

'I've always created trouble for you, haven't I?' he said.

'Of course you haven't,' she lied. 'And now, come on,' she added, 'or we'll be completing this tour of Penhally by moonlight.'

'Which would really set the local tongues wagging, wouldn't it?' he declared as he fell into step beside her. 'Audrey—'

'Forget her,' Eve ordered as they began walking back down Harbour Road, and he shook his head.

'This is a professional observation, not a personal one,' he replied. 'Her colour's very high.'

'She has angina, and she's hopeless about remembering to use her glyceryl trinitrate spray. "I keep forgetting, Nurse Dwyer",' Eve continued in a perfect imitation of Audrey's voice. 'I don't think she realises, or will accept, how serious her condition is.'

'Denial can be a form of self-protection when people are scared,' Tom observed, kicking a pebble at his feet so that it ricocheted down the street in front of them. 'If they don't think about it, it hasn't happened.'

It was true, Eve thought, but denial had never worked for her. All the denying, and pretending in the world, had never made it go away for her, and when they reached Harbour Bridge she came to a halt.

'Tom, why did you come back?' she asked. 'You always said you wouldn't, so why are you here?'

For a moment she didn't think he was going to answer, then he shrugged.

'My dad's solicitor has been bending my ear about the house, wanting to know whether I want to sell it, or rent it out.'

'You didn't have to come back to Penhally for that,' she pointed out. 'You could just have told him over the phone.'

'I suppose,' he murmured as he stared down at the river Lanson flowing gently under the bridge beneath them, then he grinned. 'OK, you've rumbled me. I thought it might be interesting to see Penhally again.'

He wasn't telling her the truth. She didn't know how she knew that, but she did.

'Tom—'

'What happened to the cinema?' he interrupted. 'It used to be up there, in Gull Close, didn't it, on the right-hand side of the river?'

'It was on the left-hand side of the river, in Bridge Street, but it closed down years ago,' she replied, all too aware that he was changing the subject, but she had secrets so she supposed he was entitled to secrets, too. 'People gradually stopped wanting to go so much once they had television in their own homes.'

'I took you to see *RoboCop*.'

'No, you didn't.'

'I did, too,' he insisted as they began walking again. 'I remember us kissing in the back row.'

'Must have been someone else. Come to think of it,' she added wryly, 'it undoubtedly *was* someone else considering you were Penhally's answer to Casanova.'

'I was not,' he replied, the grin reappearing on his face.

'Yes, you were!' she exclaimed. 'Even when we were at school, every girl fancied you like mad despite you having the most dreadful reputation.'

'You didn't.'

Oh, but I did, I *did*, she thought, but you never noticed me. It was only when you came back from med school that summer that you realised I was alive.

'That's the Penhally Bay Surgery,' she continued, deliberately changing the conversation, and Tom let out a low whistle as his gaze took in the large building to the left of the Serpentine Steps.

'I remember when the doctor's surgery was that pokey little place in Morwenna Road,' he observed.

'Nick's made big changes since he took over the practice,' Eve replied. 'And he's making even more, as you can see,' she added, pointing to the scaffolding at the back of the surgery. 'In less than a week Lauren will have a state-of-the-art physiotherapy suite, and we'll have an X-ray room, and even more consulting rooms.'

'Well, he may have grown into a grumpy old so-and-so,' Tom said, 'but at least he wants the best for his patients.'

'He does,' Eve said, 'but you haven't told me anything about yourself, your work with Deltaron.'

'Not much to tell,' he said.

'There's bound to be,' she said, but he wasn't listening to her. He was already crossing the road, heading for the children's play park and playing field. 'Tom, where are you going?'

'I fancy a swing,' he shouted back, and though she shook her head she followed him.

'Big kid,' she said when she'd caught up with him.

'You'd better believe it,' he replied, then frowned slightly as he looked up at the new houses on the hill, then down at the older buildings clustered round the harbour. 'It's odd, but it seems so much smaller than I remembered it.'

'Hicksville. That's what you used to call Penhally,' she said. '"There's a whole world out there, Eve, and I want to see it, be a part of it."'

'Did I say that?' he said dryly. 'Yeah, well, I guess I always was a stupid kid.'

She stared at him for a second, then sat down on the swing next to his.

'Tom, what's wr—?'

'You wanted to know about my work with Deltaron,' he interrupted. 'There's almost fifty of us in the organisation, but normally we'll send in around fourteen people who are specialists in the sorts of conditions we're likely to encounter.'

'What sort of specialists?' she asked.

'Let's say we're going into an earthquake situation,' he declared. 'In that case, we'd want people who are familiar with the construction of buildings, plus experts in flammable and explosive materials, electricians, pilots, plumbers and medics.'

'And when you go into a disaster area, you're in charge.'

'Yup,' he said. 'I decide where we start looking for survivors, and I decide when we quit. When there's no point in looking any more.'

A harshness had crept into his voice, and his eyes... They had become bleak, empty, and desolate.

'It must be heart-breaking at times,' she suggested tentatively, and saw his jaw tighten.

'Bleeding hearts need not apply, that's for sure.'

'Tom...' She put her hand on his arm. 'Tom, are you OK?'

He stood up abruptly, letting the swing bang back against his calves, and faked a smile.

'Couldn't be better,' he said, 'and isn't that your little friend?'

For a second Eve continued to stare at him, then she glanced in the direction of his gaze, and saw Tassie running along the road, her blonde hair flying.

'She'll be going home,' she said. 'Tom, are you quite sure you're—?'

'What's the connection between you two?'

'None,' she said, getting to her feet, and leading the way out of the play park, 'apart from the fact I've taken an interest in her since she was about four years old. Her mother, Amanda... She's had to bring up five of a family virtually on her own so I help out by looking after Tassie one day a week.'

'Isn't there a Mr Lovelace?'

'He's in prison at the moment for petty theft. I'm afraid it always is petty theft with him, or selling on stolen goods.' Eve sighed. 'The whole family are completely out of control, including Tassie's twin brother, Terry, but Gary Lovelace is the worst. Seventeen years old, and already a complete and utter waste of space.'

Tom's eyebrows rose.

'It's not like you to write off someone when they're so young.'

Eve struggled with herself for a moment, then blurted out, 'Do you remember me telling you Reverend Kenner had a daughter? Well, she's pregnant, Tom. Rachel is just seventeen years old, and pregnant by Gary Lovelace.'

'Accidents happen, Eve,' Tom declared. 'You know that.'

'This was no accident,' she retorted. 'Rachel told Chloe MacKinnon it wasn't. Gary deliberately went after Rachel because he thought it would be fun to play around with the minister's daughter. What kind of boy does that, Tom? He's no job—no desire to get one—just hangs about with his friends… He—'

'Sounds exactly like I was at his age,' Tom interrupted, and Eve shook her head vehemently.

'You were nothing like Gary.'

'Hell, Eve, I was *exactly* like Gary,' Tom protested. 'God knows what would have become of me if it hadn't been for Gertie Stanbury.'

'Our old headmistress?' Eve exclaimed. 'What did she have to do with anything?'

'Do you remember the day when the bicycle sheds burned down at school, and I swore blind I didn't do it? Well, I did, and Gertie knew I did though she couldn't prove it. She called me into her office and said, "Cornish, you can either spend the rest of your life destroying things, or you can make something of yourself. Your father—and most of Penhally—have written you off, but you've got brains and ability, so are you going to prove your father and Penhally right, or show them they're wrong?"'

Eve shook her head in amazement. 'You never told me any of this.'

'Well, it was hardly my finest hour,' Tom said wryly. 'I was furious with Gertie—thought she was an interfering old bat, to be honest—but when I went home that night, and found my father lying dead drunk as usual on the sitting-room floor, I suddenly realised I was going to be him in a few years if I didn't knuckle down at school, and get some qualifications.'

'Which is what I want Tassie to do,' she declared, 'to get some qualifications. She's such a bright child, Tom, and Gertrude has been helping her by lending her books—'

'Gertie Stanbury is still alive?'

'Very much so.' Eve nodded. 'She thinks Tassie is clever enough to win a scholarship to the Lady Joan Mercer's Boarding School in Devon which would be wonderful because though Amanda wants what's best for Tassie she'll never be able to afford to let her stay on at school once she reaches leaving age.'

'And if she does go to this school?'

Eve smiled.

'At the moment Tassie wants to become a doctor. Of course, she'll probably change her mind, but if I can get her into Lady Joan's, and she studies hard, the world will be her oyster.'

A slight frown appeared on Tom's forehead.

'You do realise if you send Tassie off to this private boarding school, she'll lose her own family?'

'Of course she won't.'

'She will,' Tom insisted. 'She'll have nothing in common with them, could even end up looking down on them, while they'll simply think she's got above herself.'

'You're saying I'm wrong—I shouldn't encourage her,' Eve exclaimed, anger rising in her.

'I'm saying…' Tom stopped and rubbed the back of his neck awkwardly with his fingers. 'I'm saying Tassie's not your daughter, Eve.'

'I know that.' Eve flared. 'I know she isn't mine, but what's so wrong about me wanting her to have every opportunity?'

'Nothing,' Tom replied gently, 'just so long as she, and her mother, and you, understand it will come at a price.'

He was wrong, Eve thought furiously as she gazed at him. Tassie wouldn't lose her family, and when she thought of all the things the girl would gain…

'I have to go,' she said, her voice tight as she stepped back from him.

'Already?' he protested. 'But I thought we could have dinner together.'

'I can't.'

'Then what about tomorrow?' he declared. 'We could drive up to Newquay—'

'You're leaving tomorrow,' she reminded him, 'and I have to work.'

'Couldn't you ask for a few days off?' he demanded. 'Even just one day?'

It was clearly important to him that she said yes, but she had no intention of saying yes. She'd agreed to today but even during the few short hours they'd spent together he'd unsettled her so much, and she'd had enough unsettling.

'Tom, I can't,' she said. 'I've only just started work at the practice so it would hardly look professional if I took time off.'

'Then this is goodbye,' he said, making it a statement, not a question, and she stuck out her hand.

'It's been nice seeing you again, Tom.'

'Eve…'

He'd taken her hand in his, his eyes intent, earnest, and he was clearly hoping she would change her mind, but he was too late. Twenty years too late, and she pulled her hand free.

'Goodbye, Tom,' she said.

And she walked away from him, and she didn't look back.

# CHAPTER THREE

'SOPHIE, tell me this isn't true?' Eve declared, gazing in horror at the sullen teenager.

'Look, I just miscalculated my insulin dose, OK?' Sophie Banks retorted belligerently. 'That's why my blood-sugar levels are all haywire today. I just made a *mistake*.'

'Mistake, my foot!' Sophie's mother exclaimed, her face tight, her eyes angry. 'I thought it was strange the way she kept rushing off to the bathroom, even wondered if she'd perhaps caught a chill, and then I heard her—bold as brass—on the phone to her friend last night, talking about this internet site she'd found—'

'You had no right to listen in to my private phone calls,' Sophie declared, outrage plain in her voice. 'I don't listen to yours—'

'Sophie, I know you weren't happy when you started putting on weight after your diabetes was diagnosed,' Eve interrupted quickly, seeing the mother and daughter round on one another, 'but skipping, or lessening your dosage in order to excrete more urine and stay thin is a recipe for disaster.'

'None of my clothes fit any more,' the teenager protested, 'I look *gross*.'

Or like a perfectly normal fifteen-year-old, Eve thought, but there was no point in saying that.

'Sophie, your weight gain is purely temporary,' she said instead. 'Once we get your blood-sugar levels under control, your weight will return to what it was before.'

'Yeah, right,' Sophie muttered under her breath, and Eve sat forward in her seat.

'This internet site you found,' she declared. 'Did it tell you that not only would you lose weight if you manipulated your insulin doses, you could also damage your eyes, and develop hypoglycaemia?'

'One mistake,' the girl said mutinously. 'All I did was make one lousy miscalculation, and now you all think I have a problem. I don't have a problem.'

Eve didn't believe her. Alison had warned her before she'd gone off on her maternity leave that Sophie seemed more interested in her weight loss than the fact she had diabetes, and when she'd tested the girl's blood-sugar levels this morning they'd been appalling. She didn't doubt for a second that Sophie had been deliberately skipping doses but warning the girl that she was, quite literally, dicing with death would achieve nothing. To a teenager, death was something that happened to other people, elderly people.

'I'm going to have a word with Dr Tremayne,' she declared. 'I'm sorry, Sophie,' she continued as the girl let out a hiss of irritation, 'but your temporary weight gain is clearly worrying you, so I think you should see an endocrinologist who will be able to advise you on your diet.'

And who will also be considerably more experienced than I am in dealing with eating disorders and diabetes, Eve added mentally.

Mrs Banks shot her daughter a that-will-sort-you-out-young-lady look, but, instead of getting to her feet and leaving as Eve had expected, the mother suddenly cleared her throat, her eyes sparkling with keen interest.

'I happened to meet Audrey Baxter on my way down to the surgery this morning, Nurse, and she said—'

Here it comes, Eve thought grimly. I thought I might have got away with it, but here it comes.

'She saw you and Tom Cornish on the beach yesterday.'

'That's right,' Eve said with the biggest smile she could muster. 'Now, as regards Sophie,' she continued determinedly. 'Hopefully, she won't have to wait long to see the endocrinologist, but until she gets an appointment I'd like to see her twice a week from now on to check on her blood-sugar levels.'

That Mrs Banks considered her a singularly disappointing source of information was plain. That she was itching to delve deeper into Tom Cornish's presence was even plainer but, unlike Audrey Baxter, Mrs Banks clearly possessed some scruples because she got to her feet, albeit reluctantly.

'We'll see you on Thursday, then, Nurse,' she said, then trooped out of Eve's consulting room, with Sophie trailing belligerently behind her, and Eve sighed wearily as she closed the teenager's folder.

*Well, what did you expect?* a little voice whispered in her mind. *When Audrey saw you in Tom's arms she was bound to spread the word, wasn't she?*

Yes, but couldn't she have kept quiet, just for once? she thought wistfully.

*Fat chance in Penhally, Eve.*

She could almost hear Tom saying that, and a smile curved her lips for a second then faded.

He'd be on his way to London now, back to the new life he'd made for himself, and their trip down memory lane was over. And that was all it had been, she reminded herself. One sunny October afternoon spent reminiscing about their youth although it had been strange how much Tom had wanted to look back. The Tom she had known had been forever planning, scheming, looking to the future, but this Tom… And he had no need to look back. He had it all right now, in the present.

'Eve, Mrs Baxter came in for a repeat prescription this morning,' Nick declared as he stuck his head round her examination-room door, 'and her BP's haywire again.'

'Like Sophie Banks's blood-sugar levels,' she replied, and when she told him what she suspected the teenager of doing Nick shook his head.

'Of all the stupid... What is it with women nowadays that so many of you want to look like stick insects?'

'I suppose it's the models we see in magazines and on television,' Eve observed. 'They're all extremely thin.'

'Idiots, the lot of them,' Nick declared. 'I'll send a letter to the endocrinology department right away, but you'd better keep an eye on her. The last thing we want is her going hypoglycaemic on us. Can you fit Mrs Baxter into your Thursday clinic, to check her BP for me again?'

'Unfortunately, yes,' Eve said dryly, and a rare smile appeared on Nick's lips.

'I know she can be a nosy old bat at times, but there's no malice in her.' The senior partner half withdrew, then paused. 'Tom gone, has he?'

The question sounded casual, indifferent, but Eve wasn't deceived.

'He left this morning,' she replied. 'Back to London, or it could have been Switzerland. I didn't ask.'

'Right.' Nick nodded, then seemed to come to a decision. 'It's better this way, Eve. It might not seem like it at the moment, but the past is simply that. Something over, done with, and attempting to recapture it can only be a mistake, especially—' his eyes met hers '—in the circumstances.'

He remembered, she thought, staring up at him, drymouthed. It had been one consultation all those years ago. Nick had been her GP even then while working in a practice in a town nearby. He must have seen hundreds of patients since, and yet he remembered, and not just remembered, had put two and two together and come up with the right answer. Not the whole answer, not the complete answer, but the right one.

'Nick…'

'Practice meeting in ten minutes, OK?'

She dredged up a smile, but when he'd gone she shut her eyes tightly. She should have gone to another doctor. She had, at the beginning. At the beginning she'd gone up to Bude because she hadn't wanted anyone to know, but then she'd caught an infection, and she'd had to go to Nick. A prescription for antibiotics, had been all she'd asked for, and when he'd examined her he hadn't said anything so she'd thought he hadn't realised, but he had. For all these years he'd known, and she couldn't bear the fact he'd known.

'Eve, do you have Stephanie Richards's file?'

Eve looked up with difficulty to see Kate standing in her doorway, and shook her head. 'Sorry, no, I don't.'

'Blast.' The midwife frowned. 'She's been on the phone—panicking again—and I thought I'd drop in on her after the practice meeting, but I wanted to check what her BP was the last time it was taken.'

'Can't help you—sorry. Maybe Dragan has the file,' Eve declared, and Kate tilted her head to one side.

'You OK?'

Eve didn't feel OK. She'd tossed and turned last night, her dreams plagued by memories she didn't want to have, and now to discover Nick knew…

'I'm fine,' she managed. 'And we,' she added, glancing down at her watch, and picking up her folders, 'had better get our skates on, or Nick will have our guts for garters for being late.'

He didn't. In fact, when Kate and Eve arrived in his consulting room, Nick was poring over plans laid out on his desk with Dragan Lovak, Oliver Fawkner, Chloe and Lauren.

'So, I should be able to move into my new physiotherapy unit by the end of the week?' Eve heard Lauren declare. 'Excellent.'

'Is Dr Devereux having one of the new consulting rooms when he arrives?' Oliver asked, and, when Nick nodded, the young doctor grinned. 'Which means Lauren will have the French charmer not only living next door to her, but also working beside her.'

'He's rented the Manor House, Oliver,' Lauren protested. 'That hardly makes him living "next door" to me.'

'Maybe you could drop in on him with a pot of soup when he arrives, make him feel welcome,' he replied slyly, and the physiotherapist shook her head at him.

'And maybe I won't.'

'And maybe we should remember this is a post-practice meeting, and not a dating agency,' Nick declared, rolling up the plans on his desk.

The consulting room became instantly silent, and Eve saw Oliver roll his eyes at Chloe, while Lauren exchanged a resigned look with Dragan. Only Kate was frowning quite openly at Nick, but he was completely ignoring her, and Eve sighed inwardly. Good doctor though Nick was, he really did need to lighten up. Tom would have handled the situation quite differently. He would have understood that sometimes they all needed to be a bit silly to relieve the stress of their jobs, but Nick either couldn't—or wouldn't—see it.

'OK, let's get down to business,' Nick continued. 'Eve, are your influenza inoculation clinics ready to roll next week?'

She nodded. 'I noticed from Alison's notes that the practice only had a 67 per cent take up rate last year.'

'Getting people to come in is proving difficult,' he conceded, 'but it *is* worthwhile particularly for those at high risk, like the elderly and those who suffer from asthma and bronchitis. We can't afford to ship them all off to drier climates for the winter.'

To places like Switzerland, Eve thought. It had a drier climate, despite the snow it got in winter. Tom had said he had a home overlooking Lake Geneva. She'd never been there—had never been abroad, full stop. She'd always meant to travel, but somehow—

'How's her BP?'

Eve felt a hot wash of colour creep over her cheeks. Dragan was gazing at her expectantly, and she didn't have a clue what he was talking about, and it was all Tom's fault. She had to get him out of her thoughts. He had gone, and he wasn't ever going to come back, so she had to stop this, and stop it now.

'I'm sorry,' she was forced to say, 'but whose BP are you talking about?'

She felt, rather than saw, Nick stiffen with disapproval, but Dragan merely smiled.

'My mind is always a bit of a sieve on Monday mornings, too,' he declared kindly. 'Lizzie Chamberlain. I saw her coming out of your room, and she looked decidedly stressed.'

'She is,' Eve replied, smiling gratefully at him. 'Her blood pressure is still way too high, but she's so worried about her mother. I know you all felt Lizzie needed a break, that nursing her mother was making her ill, but she's got it into her head that by agreeing to her mum temporarily going into the Harbour View Nursing Home she's abandoned her.'

'I have to say Mrs Chamberlain isn't doing nearly as well in there as I'd hoped,' Dragan admitted. 'I thought she might see it as a mini-holiday, but the last time I saw her she seemed very lethargic, and not really interested in anything.'

'It's a Catch-22 situation,' Eve observed. 'Nursing someone with Parkinson's is exhausting, but if Lizzie's feeling guilty, as she obviously is…'

'Would you like me to drop in on Mrs Chamberlain?' Lauren declared. 'I'm on home visits today, and I could see her before I call in on Harry Discombe in Gow Court. It wouldn't be a bother.'

Both Eve and Dragan nodded their agreement and, to Eve's relief, Oliver then launched into an account of the patients he'd seen that morning, leaving her with nothing to do but simply appear interested.

And she *was* interested, she told herself as she constantly found her mind wandering. She loved her work—always had done—so why did she feel all unsettled, and shaken up, like leaves in an autumn gale, or the flakes of snow in a snow globe, tumbling everywhere?

Because Tom came back, her mind whispered, and unconsciously she shook her head. It was over. It had been over a long time ago.

'No prizes for guessing who he's phoning.' Chloe chuckled when they all trooped out of Nick's consulting room, and Dragan immediately extracted his mobile phone from his pocket.

'I think it's sweet the way he keeps checking on Melinda, to see if she's OK,' Kate protested.

'Melinda doesn't,' Chloe said as Dragan disappeared into his room. 'I think the words, "He's driving me crazy" were the ones she used last week when she came in for her prenatal check-up. In fact, she's actually started turning off her mobile so she can get some peace and quiet.'

'No—really?' Kate laughed. 'Well, I'm off. I'll be in Bridge Street, if anyone needs me, reassuring Stephanie Richards—yet again—that her symptoms are perfectly normal, and she'll have a lovely, healthy baby in a couple of weeks' time.'

'And I'll be home if I'm needed,' Chloe declared, then shook her head as Oliver's eyes lit up. 'Defrosting the fridge, so you can forget any ideas about slipping home for a cup of coffee.'

'Coffee wasn't what I had in mind, babe,' he murmured, and the midwife chuckled, and he laughed and, as they walked away together, Eve felt her heart twist slightly.

The young couple were so much in love. Tom hadn't been in love with her, she thought sadly as she tightened her grip on the pile of folders she was carrying and started walking towards Reception.

'Let's have fun' was all he'd said that summer, and for him their romance had simply been that, a bit of fun, whereas for her... She had loved him so much, and when he'd left, when he hadn't phoned, had sent her only those two postcards, she'd felt as though her heart had been ripped out and trampled on.

'Oh, damn, blast and bloody hell!' she exclaimed as she rounded the corner and cannoned straight into someone coming the other way, sending the folders she was holding clattering to the floor.

'Language, Nurse Dwyer, *language*.'

It couldn't be, she thought, feeling her heart give an almighty leap, but as she looked up and met a pair of sparkling green eyes she saw that it was.

'You're not supposed to be here,' she blurted out before she could stop herself, and Tom grinned.

'Decided to stay on for a few more days. Thought I'd let the local garage mend my broken indicator light, make it easier for your physio.'

Pathetic, she thought as she stared up at him, wondering how he could possibly manage to look quite so heart-tinglingly handsome in an old, threadbare blue sweater and a pair of jeans. That was the most pathetic reason for staying on in Penhally she'd ever heard, but she had no intention of calling him on it. Calling him on it might mean he'd give her the real reason, and something told her she was better off not knowing the real reason.

'I'm afraid Lauren isn't here,' she said, getting down on her hands and knees to begin retrieving the files. 'She's just gone out on her home visits.'

'I didn't want to see Lauren,' he replied, hunkering down beside her. 'I wanted to see you.'

'Me?' she said faintly.

'I wondered if you'd like to come out to lunch with me?'

'Lunch?' she repeated, and his green eyes twinkled.

'As in food. A substance which sustains every living thing,' he said.

'I know what lunch is,' she protested. 'I just…' Absently, she reached for the last file, just as Tom did, too, and when their hands touched she snatched hers away quickly, all too aware that a disconcerting crackle of heat had raced up her arm. 'I just…'

'Is there a problem here?'

Eve glanced over her shoulder to see Nick standing behind her, his expression colder and stonier than she'd ever seen it.

'No problem,' she mumbled. 'Tom…he's decided to stay on for a few more days.'

'So I see,' Nick replied.

'I was also hoping to entice Eve out to lunch,' Tom declared. 'You do allow your staff to have lunch, I presume?'

'Naturally,' Nick said, his voice every bit as tight as Tom's. 'But it's my staff's choice as to who they eat that lunch with.'

And frankly I'd be happier if Eve had lunch with Genghis Khan.

Nick didn't say those words, he didn't have to. His whole body language said it for him, and although Eve now knew why the senior partner was being so antagonistic towards Tom, she didn't need—or want—him protecting her.

'It's all right, Nick,' she said, and for a second she thought the senior partner might actually argue with her, then he nodded and walked abruptly away.

'What *is* it with that guy?' Tom demanded. 'We haven't seen one another in years, and yet every time we meet it's obvious he'd dearly like to stick a knife in me.'

'Personality clash, maybe?' Eve suggested evasively. 'Give me a couple of minutes to offload these with Hazel,' she continued quickly, indicating the folders in her arms, 'and to change out of my uniform, and I'll be right with you.'

And it would be only a few minutes, she thought as she

handed the folders to their practice manager. Any longer, and she dreaded to think what Nick might come back and say.

But it wasn't Nick who was uppermost in her mind when she went into the ladies' cloakroom to change out of her uniform and saw how flushed her cheeks were, how bright her eyes. She should have looked angry, horrified, because Tom hadn't left, but the truth was she looked more alive than she had in years, and she closed her eyes to shut out the image.

What was happening to her? Just two short days ago she'd had a life. OK, so maybe it hadn't been the world's most exciting life, but she'd had her patients, and Tassie, and she'd been in control and content, and yet now...

She couldn't still have feelings for Tom, not after all these years. He'd left her without a second's thought, and though she'd been heartbroken for a long time she'd eventually picked up the pieces of her life, had dated other men. Dammit, she'd even got engaged once.

*But you broke off the engagement*, her mind whispered.

Only because I realised it was a mistake, she argued back. That it would be wrong to marry someone, and keep secrets from him. It wasn't because I still had feelings for Tom.

*Oh, really?* Her mind laughed, and she gripped the edge of the sink tightly.

Somehow, some way, she had to pull herself together. Somehow, some way, she had to keep her emotions in check, because she couldn't go down that road again, Nick had been right about that. Recapturing the past would mean resurrecting it, and she couldn't do that, not ever.

'Eve, we were just talking about you,' Dragan said when Eve emerged from the ladies' cloakroom to find him and Tom laughing about something.

'Saying something nice, I hope?' Eve said lightly, and Dragan smiled.

'Tom was telling me about his home in Lausanne, and I was

saying he must take you there some time. It's a beautiful part of Switzerland.'

'You know it?' Eve asked, deliberately sidestepping the suggestion that she would want Tom to take her anywhere.

'I do, indeed,' Dragan observed. 'When I was young, my family and I went there a couple of times for holidays before… Before everything changed.'

A shadow had appeared in his eyes, and Eve knew the Croatian doctor was remembering happier times when his homeland hadn't been torn by war, when all of his family had been safe, and alive.

'Dragan,' she began hesitantly, and he shook his head and forced a smile.

'Sometimes it's good to remember the past, and sometimes it's not,' he said. 'But you must let Tom take you to Switzerland. It truly is a beautiful place.'

'I'm sure it is,' Eve said, then added quickly when she saw Tom open his mouth, clearly intending to interrupt, 'How's Melinda?'

'Tired,' Dragan admitted. 'Tired of waiting, tired of looking—she says—like a hot-air balloon that's about to go pop.'

Eve laughed.

'At least she hasn't got much longer to go,' she said. 'Just two more weeks, and then you'll be a proud papa.'

'Do you know whether it's a boy or a girl?' Tom asked, and Dragan shook his head.

'Melinda and I didn't want to know. We wanted it to be a surprise. And speaking of surprises,' he added, glancing at his watch, and letting out a muttered oath, 'if I don't get my home visits started the only surprise will be me managing to have them finished by midnight.'

'Brave man,' Tom observed as Dragan hurried away, 'coming to the UK, making himself a new life in a foreign land.'

'It wasn't easy for him—not at first,' Eve replied, 'but then he met Melinda, and…' She smiled. 'The rest, as they say, is history.'

'What I don't understand is why I keep feeling I know him from somewhere,' Tom said. 'I thought the same thing when I met him and his wife at the reception on Saturday, but I can't for the life of me figure out why.'

And I'm not about to jog your memory, Eve thought as she slipped on her jacket, and led the way out of the surgery. Melinda and Dragan had endured more than enough harassment back in April when their photographs had been plastered all over the newspapers, and they were entitled to some privacy.

'Where do you want to have lunch?' she said, deliberately changing the subject.

'I thought maybe The Grape Seed.'

'I'm afraid it closed down years ago,' she replied as they began walking up the road past the surfing and souvenir shops, skirting the puddles left from the thunderstorm that had deluged the village earlier that morning. 'When Mr Forrest retired, his son didn't want to take it over, so it became an estate agent's.'

'Damn!' Tom exclaimed. 'I loved The Grape Seed. Remember when you could choose all those different sorts of salad dishes, like grated carrot mixed with coconut, curried eggs, and pasta salad with tuna, and we thought we were the height of sophistication?'

Eve smiled and nodded, but she wished he'd stop this. She didn't want to keep dwelling on the past. It was over, gone.

'We could have lunch at the Anchor?' she suggested, and he shook his head.

'Too stuffy. I always feel as though they're itching to check my pockets for cutlery after I eat there.'

She let out a small snort of laughter.

'We could just buy some tortilla wraps, and eat them down by the harbour,' she said, then glanced up at the sky. 'And, then again, perhaps not. I think it's going to rain again.'

And it would be yet more heavy rain. The sea might currently be a sheet of near-Mediterranean blue, and the houses and steep roads that made up Penhally Bay might be standing out in sharp relief against the cliffs behind, but she could see another band of black clouds gathering over the cliffs.

'What's that café like?' Tom asked, inclining his head towards it.

'They do very nice soups, and puddings, and if you want something a bit more substantial—'

'*Lovak!*' Tom exclaimed, coming to a sudden halt in the middle of the pavement. 'Melinda and Dragan *Lovak*. She's that European princess. The one who gave up her throne to marry the Croatian refugee.'

Eve sighed. 'So it reached the London newspapers, did it?'

'It reached *every* newspaper, Eve.' Tom shook his head in disbelief. 'I should have recognised them immediately.'

Eve wished he hadn't recognised the couple at all.

'Tom, as far as Melinda is concerned, she's Mrs Lovak, the local vet, and a soon-to-be mum,' she said. 'And as far as Dragan is concerned, he's simply one of the Penhally doctors.'

'I can see why,' Tom observed. 'I wouldn't want my past splashed all over the papers. You'd be OK with your blameless history, but me…' He laughed. 'I doubt if my bosses would be overjoyed to learn I burned down bicycle sheds when I was at school.'

And he'd somehow put his foot in it again, Tom thought as he saw Eve's face set. He'd only been making a joke at his own expense, and yet the shutters had quite clearly come down and he could almost feel her physically withdrawing from him.

'Is Dragan taking paternity leave after his wife's given birth?' he continued quickly. 'I know I would be if I were in his shoes.'

'Yes, he's taking paternity leave.'

And that hadn't helped at all, he realised, seeing her face set into even more rigid lines. *OK, change the subject*, he told himself. *Talk about something else—somebody else.*

'I met your minister on the way down here—Reverend Kenner,' he declared. 'He had his daughter, Rachel, with him. Nice kid. When's her baby due?'

'December.'

Which didn't seem to please Eve any more than his comments about Dragan and Melinda had, he thought with a sigh.

'Look, I know you're not happy about the situation,' he said. 'Her being only being seventeen, and Gary Lovelace being the father, but I've always been a very firm advocate of a woman's right to choose. She didn't have to go ahead and have the baby, Eve. She could have opted for a termination, but she didn't. Her decision, her choice, and I admire her for it.'

Eve clearly didn't if her complete silence as she led the way into the café was anything to go by, and Tom groaned as he followed her.

Hell, was he always going to be fated to somehow inadvertently say the wrong thing? Maybe he should just have gone back to London this morning, but he hadn't wanted to leave, hadn't wanted the last words they'd exchanged to have been remote and distant ones.

*And was that the only reason you didn't want to leave?* his mind whispered, and he sighed.

He wished it was. It would have made things so much easier, but he'd spent the last twenty years of his life trying to convince himself he'd done the right thing only to have that illusion blown straight out of the water the minute he'd seen her again. All it had taken was one smile from her and the great weight that had been lying on his heart for so long had suddenly lifted and the world no longer seemed such a dark and empty place.

But how to tell her this? he wondered as they sat down at a table, and both picked up a menu. How to confess he'd made a mistake all those years ago?

'Eve—'

'I'll have the carrot and coriander soup, then lemon meringue pie, please,' she told the smiling waitress who had appeared at their table.

'The same for me,' Tom said, not bothering to look at the menu. He glanced around at the café as the waitress bustled away. 'Nice place,' he continued awkwardly. 'I'm surprised we're the only customers.'

'They'll be closing at the end of the week,' Eve replied. 'They haven't gone bankrupt, or anything,' she added. 'A lot of the restaurants, and most of the craft and gift shops, in Penhally close down at the end of the summer. It's not really viable for them to stay open over the winter.'

'Right,' he said, then cleared his throat. 'I want to apologise to you for what I said about Tassie yesterday. I don't know the family—don't even know the girl—so I spoke out of turn.'

'Yes, you did.'

Which pretty well finished that as a topic of conversation, he thought.

'It's raining again,' he ventured, as he stared out of the café window looking for inspiration. 'And the Lanson's running pretty high.'

'We had a lot of rain this morning,' Eve replied. 'We often do in October.'

And I'm dying a death here, Tom thought ruefully, if we're reduced to talking about the weather. Hell's teeth, it shouldn't be this hard to start a conversation, and keep it going. All he had to do was not mention Tassie Lovelace, Melinda and Dragan Lovak, Rachel Kenner or Eve's parents, and surely he'd be on safe ground.

'*Dirty Dancing*,' he said quickly. 'I've just remembered the film I took you to see at the old La Scala was *Dirty Dancing*, and you made me see it three times because you had a thing about Patrick Swayze.'

'It wasn't so much Patrick Swayze,' Eve said as the waitress appeared with their soup. 'It was more… I think I liked the film because it was about trying to fulfil your dreams.'

'Don't tell me you actually sit down and watch it when it comes on TV?' He laughed, and saw her jaw set as she picked up her spoon.

'No. I don't.'

*OK*, he thought. Let's try something else.

'Do you remember—?'

'Stop it, Tom.'

Her large brown eyes were unexpectedly hard, and he gazed at her in confusion. 'Stop what?'

'All these reminiscences, this trip down memory lane. We're not in our twenties any more. We've both moved on, we're different people now.'

'I don't think you've changed very much from the person I once knew,' he said with a smile, and she shook her head.

'You didn't even know me twenty years ago, Tom, not really.'

'Of course I did,' he protested, then glanced over his shoulder to see where their waitress was. 'Hell, Eve, we were lovers. If anybody knows you, it's me.'

'You might have known my body,' she said quietly. 'But you didn't know me.'

'You're talking in riddles,' he replied. 'Of course I knew you. Just as I also feel…' He lowered his voice still further. 'The old attraction between us… It's still there, isn't it?'

A peal of thunder had rung out, followed by a jagged fork of lightning, but Eve ignored them both and put down her spoon, cynicism and anger plain in her eyes.

'What you're feeling is a desire for the past, Tom,' she replied, 'for when your life was simpler. It's isn't me you want back. It's your youth.'

Was she right? he wondered as he stared back at her and unconsciously he shook his head. It was more than that, so much more than that.

'If you're saying I want to be young again, then the answer's no,' he replied. 'If I could go back, knowing what I know now, that would be different, but to go back to the thoughtless man I was then…' He reached out and clasped her hand. 'All I do know is I never forgot you.'

'Your never forgetting me didn't extend to you keeping in touch, did it?' she exclaimed, pulling her hand free, and he winced at the hardness in her voice. 'Two postcards, Tom. Two lousy, miserable postcards. One saying you were lonely, the other saying you had applied for a job with Deltaron, and then nothing.'

'I meant to write,' he began hesitantly, 'but the longer I was away, the more—'

'You forgot about me?' she finished for him, and he dragged his fingers through his hair.

'No,' he protested. 'I just thought—as the years passed—you'd be bound to be married—have a family.'

'And now you've discovered I'm not, you think it might be nice to try to pick up where you left off,' she said, her voice brittle. 'Well, you can forget it, Tom.'

'Eve—'

'Something wrong with the soup?' the waitress interrupted, appearing without warning at their table, and glancing from Eve's scarcely touched bowl to Tom's.

'It's lovely—perfect,' Tom said with an effort.

'Better than the weather.' The waitress laughed as another peal of thunder rang out and rain began bouncing onto the street outside, filling the drains and gullies so quickly they started to overflow.

'Eve, I didn't come back to resurrect the past,' Tom said the second the waitress had gone. 'I came back for two reasons. One I can tell you about, the other…' He shook his head. 'I can't tell you that, not just yet.'

'Then tell me the one reason you can,' she said, folding her arms across her chest with a look on her face that said all too plainly, you'd better make this good.

'I came back because…' He took an uneven breath. 'I wanted to see if I could still feel anything. Even if all I felt in Penhally was the old resentment, the old hatred, at least it would mean I could still feel *something*.'

Eve gazed at him, open-mouthed. Whatever she had been expecting him to say, it hadn't been that.

'I…I don't understand,' she faltered, and Tom pushed his soup away.

'Eve, during the years I've worked for Deltaron, I've witnessed the most wonderful—amazing—acts of courage and self-sacrifice. I've seen men and women tear at rubble with their bare hands in a desperate attempt to rescue people they've never met, but I've also seen men and women trample on children—babies—crushing them into the mud, in order to save themselves or to grab a crust of bread.'

'I suppose disasters always bring out both the best, and the worst, in people,' she said awkwardly, and his lips twisted into a bitter smile.

'It also breeds indifference, Eve. I was in New Orleans, and Colombia, and Phuket. Horrendous, all of them, but they got help because they made the headlines, whereas in so many places—too many places—I've had to watch people die because the food, and the shelter, and the medicine never came.'

'Tom—'

'Jean Paul Sartre, the French philosopher, said Hell was other people. He was wrong, Eve. Hell is people ceasing to care.'

'But you care,' she protested, seeing the desolation in his face. 'You wouldn't be doing the job you're doing if you didn't.'

'But the trouble is…' He picked up his spoon and put it down again. 'I'm ceasing to care. Ceasing to feel anything. So a hundred people were killed a month ago, a thousand the month before that. Maybe they're better off dead rather than being rescued by my men simply to survive for another month, or a year, only to be hit by yet another catastrophe, yet another disaster, and lose more loved ones.'

It was so dark outside the café now it could almost have been night, and vaguely Eve was aware of people scurrying past the café window, hurrying to get out of the rain, but what she was most aware of was the bleak, raw despair in Tom's face. Never had she seen such utter desolation on someone's face before and, as she stared at him, she suddenly realised she was feeling an emotion she would never have believed she would ever feel for him, and it wasn't attraction, or anger, or hatred. It was pity.

'Tom, you can't—you mustn't—think like that,' she said quickly, but he didn't seem to hear her.

'So many children orphaned, Eve,' he murmured. 'So many babies, sitting in cots all over the world, who are given enough food and water to live on, but no love, no affection, because there's simply too many of them, and every year their numbers increase.'

'Tom—'

'Maybe Nick was right,' he continued with a shuddering sigh. 'Maybe my whole working life has been nothing but a series of photo opportunities.'

She caught hold of his hand and held it tightly.

'Nick was wrong,' she protested. 'Your work is vitally important.'

'Yeah, right,' he said, with a smile that tore at her heart. 'Dr Tom Cornish, head of operations for Deltaron, the big cheese, the head honcho, but, when it comes right down to it, you're the one who's made something of your life.'

'But you've made a wonderful success of your life,' she said, even more confused. 'I'm just a nurse, Tom, whereas you… There are people alive today who wouldn't be if you hadn't rescued them.'

'But at the end of the day, it's you people remember, isn't it?' he said, turning her hand over in his, and staring down at it. 'You're that nice, kind, sympathetic nurse at the surgery. The one who holds people's hands when they're scared, the one who gives them a cuddle when they need it.'

The misery in his face was palpable and she had to swallow hard before she could answer him.

'Tom, people remember you,' she declared, her voice uneven. 'You're the man who arrives whenever there's an emergency, the man who helps. What you do, it's what you always wanted to do—so how has it all gone wrong? I can see how constantly facing so much death and destruction must wear you down, but what's happened to make you feel your work—your whole life—has been pointless?'

He didn't get a chance to reply. Another peal of thunder rumbled overhead, the lights in the café flickered and went out, and the waitress bustled towards them.

'Thought as much,' she said with resignation. 'Sorry, folks, but I'm not going to be able to give you your puddings.'

'It doesn't matter,' Tom said, getting abruptly to his feet and extracting his wallet. 'We've discovered we're not very hungry.'

'I'd get home as quickly as you can if I were you,' the waitress declared as she took Tom's money. 'The Lanson's running higher than I've ever seen it.' She glanced at Eve's light jacket, and Tom's sweater and jeans. 'You'd better borrow these umbrellas or you'll both be soaked in seconds.'

The waitress was right, Eve realised when she and Tom left the café. Not only was the rain—if anything—even heavier, the Lanson was now lapping ominously close to the top of its banks.

'I don't like this,' Tom murmured as he stared at it. 'Look at the colour of the river, Eve. It's almost black, and can you smell it? That's earth—lots and lots of earth. We have to get back to the surgery, and phone the emergency services, because I think this means trouble. Big trouble.'

'The Lanson's breached its banks before,' Eve protested. 'See, people are already putting sandbags round their doors, and boarding up their shop windows. OK, so we'll probably get an inch or two of water on the pavements, but once this thunderstorm's over—'

'Eve, we have to get away from here *now*,' he interrupted.

He was overreacting, Eve told herself, shivering slightly as more thunder and lightning split the sky. Yes, the river was high—incredibly high—and it smelt and looked odd, but calling the emergency services was far too extreme.

'Tom—'

He didn't even acknowledge she had spoken. He was already hustling her down the road, but, just as they reached the bottom of Harbour Road, they both came to a halt as a sound shattered the air. A bomb or a gas explosion, was Eve's immediate thought, but the sound was immediately followed by a roar. A terrible, screaming roar that made her look over her shoulder and what she saw made her heart stop.

'Tom.' She whispered. 'Oh, my God, Tom, *look*!'

A torrent of water was cascading out of Bridge Street, completely engulfing Harbour Bridge. Engulfing it in a raging, nine-foot-high torrent of black water in which dustbins were being tossed like toys before being spat out into the harbour, and when Tom grabbed her hand she didn't hesitate for a second. She began to run.

# CHAPTER FOUR

'HAS a gas main exploded?' Hazel, the practice manager, exclaimed, her face white with shock, as Tom and Eve raced into the surgery. 'I heard this awful sound, then our landline went dead, and I've been trying to get the police on my mobile—'

'Where's Nick?' Tom demanded, cutting right across the practice manager without compunction.

'He's not here,' Hazel replied. 'Kate rang about fifteen minutes ago, saying she wasn't happy about Stephanie Richards, so he went to help her.'

'Who's Stephanie Richards?' Tom asked, looking from Eve to Hazel, but it was Eve who answered.

'Mum-to-be, due date the 20th of this month. Her boyfriend walked out on her when he discovered she was pregnant, and she's not had an easy pregnancy. She…' Eve swallowed convulsively. 'Tom… She lives in Bridge Street.'

'Not the best place to be at the moment,' Tom said evenly, and Eve let out a cry that was halfway between a sob and a laugh.

*'Not the best place?'* she repeated. 'Tom, you saw that water—'

'What the hell was that noise?' Oliver interrupted as he came running out of his consulting room. 'I was ploughing through my paperwork, listening to the rain bouncing off the roof, then it sounded as though a bomb had gone off.'

'The river Lanson's broken its banks,' Tom declared, 'and, at a rough guess, I'd say it's running nine feet higher than it should be.'

'Nine *feet*?'

'Oliver, it was awful—truly awful!' Eve exclaimed, as the young doctor stared at her, open-mouthed. 'One minute the Harbour Bridge was there, and the next…'

'You mean, the bridge has collapsed?' Oliver gasped, and Eve shook her head helplessly.

'I don't know. It might still be there, under the water, but…' She clasped her hands together to try to stop them shaking. 'Tom—Kate and Nick, and the people who live in Gull Close and Bridge Street like Gertrude Stanbury, Audrey Baxter—we have to help them. That water…'

'I know,' Tom said, his gaze steady, his voice calm, 'but we both also know we haven't a hope in hell of getting up either of those streets. Hazel, phone Nick on his mobile—'

'I can't, Tom,' the practice manager interrupted. 'Bridge Street, Gull Close and Penhally Heights—they're all blind spots as far as mobiles are concerned. I could try reaching them by radio, but if they've left their handsets in their cars…'

'We'd be better off using smoke signals,' Tom finished for her grimly. 'OK, Oliver, as Nick isn't here, you're in charge.'

'No,' the young doctor declared immediately. 'Absolutely not. Hell, Tom, you're head of operations at Deltaron. If anyone has the expertise for a situation like this, it's you.'

That Tom didn't want to be in charge was plain. A shadow had crossed his face, making him look, Eve thought, suddenly every one of his forty-four years, but Oliver was right. Only Tom had experience of dealing with this sort of situation, and whatever had happened to him, whatever he had witnessed that had made him feel he had wasted his life, it didn't alter the fact that they needed him.

'Tom?' Eve said hesitantly, and saw a small muscle clench in his cheek, then he nodded.

'All right, but one thing has to be understood,' he said. 'If I'm in charge then whatever I decide we go with, no argument, no discussion. Even if you don't like my decision—feel it's the wrong one—my decision stands.'

'I hardly think any of us are going to query your judgment,' Oliver said, and when Eve and Hazel nodded their agreement, Tom's lips curved slightly.

'I'll remind you of that later,' he said, then turned to Hazel. 'Phone the coastguard, the fire brigade, and keep phoning the police. Tell them the Lanson's broken its banks, and we need help now.' He glanced at his watch. 'It's just after two o'clock, which means the kids will still be in school. Oliver, phone both the primary and secondary schools, tell them not to let any of the children go home. Eve, I need a map of the village—the more detailed the better.'

Eve scarcely heard him. Try as she may, she couldn't forget the wall of surging, churning water, and when she thought of Audrey, and Gertrude, the people who might have been walking down those two streets… And Tassie. Her heart clutched and twisted inside her. Tassie was always calling in on Gertrude to borrow books. What if she was there, in Gull Close, trapped?

She won't be, her mind insisted. It's a school day, so Tassie will be in school, safe, and, as she felt a surge of relief course through her, she dug her fingernails deep into the palms of her hands, hating herself for feeling such relief when so many others were in danger.

'Eve, we can stand here worrying, or we can do something, and right now I need that map.'

She looked up to find Tom's gaze on her, and though there was understanding in his green eyes, there was impatience in them, too, and with an effort she straightened her shoulders.

'There's an aerial photograph of Penhally in the waiting room,' she said. 'Would that be any use?'

'Perfect,' Tom replied. 'Absolutely perfect.'

'Tom, how can this have happened?' she said as she followed him into the waiting room. 'We've had violent thunderstorms before, but never anything like this.'

'My guess is the thunderstorm earlier this morning caused something to collapse further up the hill, forming a dam,' Tom replied as he took the photograph off the wall. 'Then, when we had the second thunderstorm, the sound we heard was the dam breaking. I can't think of anything else which would cause such a volume of water to travel down at such speed.'

'Schools alerted,' Oliver announced when Tom and Eve returned to Reception, 'and I've phoned St Piran Hospital, warned them to be on standby for possible casualties.'

'The firemen are on their way,' Hazel chipped in, 'but whether they'll be able to get here is another matter. Roads seem to be flooded everywhere. The coastguard have scrambled their helicopter, and the Royal Navy are sending three more.'

'What about the police?' Tom demanded, and Hazel shook her head.

'All of their mobile phone numbers seemed to be permanently engaged. Not surprising, really, under the circumstances.'

'Keep phoning them,' Tom said. 'They need to start evacuating people in case that water spreads, and we have to find somewhere safer, too.'

'But surely we're safe here?' Eve protested. 'The water was racing straight out of Bridge Street into the harbour.'

'We need to be higher, much higher,' Tom insisted. 'Do either of the schools have a generator?'

'The high school does,' Hazel replied.

'Then the high school would be the best place for us to relocate to, and it would also be perfect for the villagers living on the west side of the Lanson to assemble,' Tom observed. 'For the people who live east of the river…' He squinted at the aerial photograph. 'The Smugglers' is the highest, and there's also fields behind it where a helicopter could land. Would there be anybody at the inn at this time of day?'

'Tony—the owner,' Eve replied. 'He's always there, and I know he'd be more than willing to help, but won't we need a medic on site in case someone comes in injured?'

'Dragan,' Tom said. 'He was going out on home visits today, wasn't he, so where's he likely to be?'

Eve picked up the home-visits notebook, and scanned it quickly.

'At a guess, I'd say he should have reached Mrs Young at Penhally Heights by now.'

'Excellent.' Tom nodded. 'Oliver…' The young doctor wasn't listening. He was punching numbers into his mobile phone, and with a flush of irritation Tom turned to Hazel. 'Phone Tony at The Smugglers', explain the situation, and then see if you get Dragan. If you do, tell him not to attempt to come back into the town, but to head for The Smugglers'. Where's your physio? Laurie—'

'Lauren,' Eve corrected him. 'She said she was dropping in on Mrs Chamberlain at Harbour View, then going on to Gow Court.'

'Where's Gow Court on this photograph?' Tom asked, and Eve pointed to it.

'It's a newly built sheltered housing complex, in this small cul-de-sac running off from Trelawney Rise.'

'Which means, if Lauren's already left the nursing home, and is on her way to Gow Court,' Tom murmured, 'she'll either be driving down Penhally View, then into Polkerris Road, and on to Gow Court, or…'

'She could have taken the quicker route down Bridge Street,' Eve said.

Tom's eyes met hers, blank, unreadable.

'Then let's hope she's taken the scenic route,' he said evenly. 'Hazel—'

'Chloe's not answering, Eve,' Oliver exclaimed in frustration. 'I've rung her over and over, and she's not picking up the phone.'

'Maybe she's asleep,' Eve declared, seeing the worry on the young doctor's face. 'Maybe she had to go out,' she continued, only to realise too late that this hadn't been the wisest wise thing to say. 'I mean—'

'I've left a message on Dragan's mobile, telling him to make for The Smugglers',' Hazel interrupted. 'I've also got Chief Constable D'Ancey on my mobile. Do you want me to tell him we've agreed on two places of safety—the high school and The Smugglers'?'

Tom nodded, and turned back to Eve. 'Does Gow Court have wardens as it's a sheltered housing complex?'

'Carol and Florry Ford,' Eve replied.

'Phone them. If Lauren's there, tell her to make straight for the school hall.'

Eve didn't say, *But what if she isn't there?* But Tom must have realised she was thinking it, because as she picked up her mobile he smiled encouragingly at her.

'One step at a time, Eve,' he said, and she managed to smile back, but she felt less like smiling when she couldn't get a reply from Gow Court, and her smile disappeared completely when the lights in the surgery began to flicker.

'I'm surprised that hasn't happened before,' Hazel observed. 'Our emergency generator will kick in but…'

'It's time for us to move,' Tom finished for her. 'Where's your radio equipment?' he continued, and when Eve led him through to the back of Hazel's office to show him, he let out a low whistle. 'I'll say one thing for Nick, he hasn't stinted on anything. OK, we need to take this, and every piece of movable medical equipment we think we might need up to the school hall. Where's Oliver?'

As though on cue, the young doctor appeared behind them, his face white with worry.

'Chloe's still not answering,' he said. 'Where is she—*where the hell is she*?'

'Oliver, you have my permission to keep phoning your fiancée,' Tom exclaimed, not bothering to hide his irritation, 'but can you do it while you're also carrying some medical equipment out to your car?'

Oliver opened his mouth, then closed it again, and grimly picked up two of their portable defibrillators and disappeared with them.

'Tom, he's worried about Chloe,' Eve said awkwardly. 'He loves her.'

'And as far as we know she's safe, whereas a lot of people in Penhally aren't,' Tom retorted, 'so can we start moving things to the hall, or are we going to wait until the Lanson is lapping round our ankles?'

He was right, Eve knew he was. Speed was of the essence, but she wished he'd been a little kinder, a little gentler, with Oliver. She would have been frantic, too, if she'd been in the young doctor's shoes, and it didn't surprise her when she saw Oliver constantly checking his phone as they moved their portable medical equipment out to their cars, and he was still attempting to contact Chloe when they were carrying it through the rain and into the school.

'She said she was going to spend the whole afternoon at home, Eve,' Oliver muttered when they began setting up the radio equipment in the small office leading off from the school hall. 'You heard her. That's where she said she would be, so *why* isn't she answering the phone?'

Eve wished she knew. She wished, even more, that she could find some words of comfort to give to the young man, but she couldn't think of anything to say apart from, *She'll be all right*, and there was no point in saying that. Oliver would quite rightly turn round and demand to know how the hell she knew, so she simply squeezed his arm, and tried to look as reassuring as she could as they finished connecting all the radio equipment.

'OK, this radio must never be left unattended,' Tom declared when he joined them. 'When our mobile batteries run out—as they assuredly will—it's going to be our only means of contacting the outside world. We'll take it in rotas, but somebody needs to be by the radio at all times.'

'I'll take the first shift,' Eve said quickly. 'I mean, I haven't exactly been of much use up until now,' she added as Hazel hurried off in answer to Oliver's beckoning wave, 'so can I take the first shift on the radio?'

'Of course you can,' Tom said, 'but what do you mean, you haven't been much use?'

Eve shrugged helplessly.

'Hazel… She's been so efficient, on the ball, and I…I just keep seeing that wall of water, thinking if anyone was walking down Bridge Street, or Gull Close, when the dam broke…'

'Considering how heavy the rain was beforehand, I should imagine most people would have hurried indoors, don't you?' he said, and she forced a smile.

'I suppose so,' she said, then bit her lip. 'How do you do it—manage to stay so calm?'

'Because it's my job,' he answered simply. 'Running around like a headless chicken isn't going to get me anywhere.'

'No,' she muttered. 'Sorry. Memo to self. Stop behaving like a headless chicken. It's just…' She shivered involuntarily as the sky outside the office window lit up with lightning. 'I'm so cold, Tom. I don't know why, but I'm so cold, and I can't seem to get warm.'

He walked towards her, and before she knew what was happening he had wrapped his arms around her.

'Shock,' he said. 'What you're suffering from is shock.'

'Is that a professional diagnosis, Dr Cornish?' she said, resting her forehead on his chest, and holding onto him because he felt warm and solid, and so very good.

'Absolutely,' he murmured into her hair. 'Are your feet dry?'

She jerked her head up to look at him. 'What?'

'Wet feet make you feel cold, and cold hands made you feel downright miserable.'

'What medical textbook did that come out off?' she said, chuckling a little unevenly.

'The Dr Tom Cornish book of medical symptoms,' he said. 'It's never ever wrong.'

She put her head back on his chest, needing his warmth, his closeness.

'Tom…I'm scared— so very scared.'

'Glad to hear it,' he said to her surprise. 'A healthy dose of fear means you're not going to be tempted to do anything stupid.'

'I've got more than a healthy dose of fear at the moment, believe me,' Eve said with feeling, 'and yet you… Doesn't anything scare you?'

'Lots of things. Spiders the size of dinner plates, crocs, boa constrictors.'

She shuddered.

'You must think I'm such a wimp,' she mumbled, and to her surprise he tilted her chin so she had to face him.

'I think you're wonderful. I always have done.'

There was tenderness in his face. An unutterable tenderness that made her heart clutch, and desperately she tried to remember all the years they'd been apart, the times when she'd been so unhappy, the reasons why she'd hated him, but all she was aware of was that—stupidly—crazily—she wanted to stay in his arms for ever.

'Do you ever wonder what would have happened if I hadn't

gone to the States?' he said as though he'd read her mind, and she tried to avoid his gaze but couldn't.

'I think it's too late for regrets, Tom,' she said, feeling her throat tighten.

'Is it?' he said. 'Eve—this flood—if anything should happen to me—'

'Don't say that,' she ordered, quickly putting her fingers to his lips to silence him, feeling a chill wrap itself round her heart at his words. 'We're safe here. Nothing is going to happen to either of us.'

'But suppose it did,' he declared. 'I just want you to know—'

Whatever he had been about to say was lost as their radio crackled into life, and a deep, male, Irish voice suddenly rang out.

'Is that idle bastard, Tom Cornish, sitting on his backside somewhere nearby?' the disembodied voice said, and Tom turned quickly towards the radio with a broad smile.

'Hey, Mad Mitch,' he said, releasing Eve to pick up the handset and press the respond button. 'What the hell are you doing there?'

A booming laugh echoed down the radio.

'Well, the Navy contacted Deltaron, said Penhally was in a bit of bother, and asked if we could help. The boys and I hummed and hawed because there was a football match on the television, but when they said our contact was someone called Tom Cornish, we knew there couldn't be two lazy buggers by that name so here we are.'

'Who in the world is that?' Eve whispered, and Tom grinned.

'Michael Finnegan, known to everyone at Deltaron as Mad Mitch because he'll fly when no sane man would.'

Another guffaw came over the radio.

'Nice to know I'm appreciated, Tom, but maybe you ought to get your lady friend to show you how to use the mute button in case I hear something I shouldn't. I tell you, mate, they could put you in a men-only changing room, and you'd still manage to find a woman.'

'He's just kidding,' Tom said, colouring slightly as Eve's eyebrows rose. 'Where are you, Mitch?'

'Coming into Penhally over the sea, and let me tell you it's horrendous out here. Rain's just running off my blades, and visibility's virtually nil. All I'm picking up is what my strobes are hitting. I've been told to head for two streets called Bridge Street and Gull Close, but, if the floodwater's as bad as we've been led to believe, you know what that could mean. OAO until we're closer to you.'

'What did he mean by, "you know what that could mean"?' Eve asked as the radio went dead.

'At the moment, the water's flowing down Bridge Street and Gull Close, and out to sea,' Tom replied. 'What Mitch is worried about is if it encounters a blockage.'

'Is that likely?' Oliver asked as he joined them.

'If buildings start to come down, then, yes, it is,' Tom declared 'All we need is a large enough tall of masonry and the water will have to find some other way out.'

'So, what you're saying is, nowhere in Penhally is safe?' Oliver exclaimed.

'Harbour View should be OK as it's high above the village, as should the two schools, and The Smugglers',' Tom replied, 'but other than that… Yes, I guess that's pretty much what I'm saying.'

'But isn't there something you can do if a building collapses?' Oliver faltered. 'Some way you can divert the water, make it flow elsewhere?'

'In an open environment there are things I could try, but in the middle of a village…' Tom shook his head. 'All we can do is hope and pray.'

'Is anyone there?'

The voice on the radio was faint, but unmistakably that of Kate Althorp, and quickly Eve lifted the handset.

'Kate, I'm here,' she said. 'Where are you?'

'Nick, are you sure this damn thing works?' she heard the midwife demand. 'All I'm getting is a lot of crackles.'

'Kate, you need to press the red button,' Eve said. 'Once you press that, you'll be able to hear me.'

'Oh. Right. Eve, is that you?' Kate said. 'Thank God. I thought… Never mind what I thought. OK, I know this is probably a non-starter,' the midwife continued, 'but we really could do with some help here. Stephanie's in labour, and it's a breech. We've no electricity, scarcely any equipment except what's in our medical bags, and we can't leave because there's about three feet of water downstairs.'

Eve glanced across at Tom, and he took the receiver from her, and sat down.

'Kate, it's Tom Cornish here. Where are you in Bridge Street?'

'Number sixteen. Luckily, it's a two-storey building, so we're upstairs, but…' They heard the midwife take a quick, and unsteady intake of breath. 'The building is shaking rather ominously, and Stephanie really does need to get to hospital, and the faster the better.'

'Can you hang a white pillowcase—something visible like that—out of the window of the room you're in so the choppers know where you are?' Tom asked.

'We can do that,' Kate replied. 'But, Tom…' The midwife took another uneven breath. 'We really do need help.'

'I know,' he said softly, then flipped the off button on the handset.

'Kate must be terrified,' Eve said as she saw him change the frequency on the radio, and knew he was trying to contact his colleague, Mad Mitch. 'Her husband—James—he drowned ten years ago, trying to rescue children who were cut off by the tide. Kate's always been scared of water, and if anything should happen to her… Her son's only nine, Tom.'

'I *know*,' Tom flared, then shook his head when Eve flinched. 'Sorry—sorry. Mitch, are you there, and if you are, where are you?'

'I'm over the harbour, Tom, and this is a bad one,' the Irish pilot declared. 'I've been talking to the coastguard pilot, and the Navy blokes, and we're all agreed. We're going to have to fly in singly, and do a snatch and grab. The access into Penhally over the harbour is too narrow, and if our blades collide…'

'Mitch, we have a woman in labour in Bridge Street,' Tom declared. 'She has two medics with her, but they've no electricity, and she needs to be in hospital pronto.'

'I hear you, Tom, but I can see people on roofs, people hanging out of windows. Men, women, children, and… Holy mackerel, part of a building's just gone. It looks like a hotel, but…' There was silence, then Mitch spoke again. 'Bob says that according to his map it's the Anchor Hotel, and the water's now spreading into…' There was another silence. 'Fisherman's Row. Bob says the water's now in Fisherman's Row.'

Eve heard Oliver's sharp intake of breath, but Tom ignored him.

'Mitch, can you see any people in danger of drowning?' he asked with a calmness that Eve could only wonder at.

'Hell, mate, I can see people everywhere in danger of drowning,' the pilot replied, and Tom's eyes met Eve's, then Oliver's.

'OK, save any children you see first,' he said.

'But, Tom,' Oliver protested. 'Chloe—'

'I repeat, Mitch,' Tom declared. 'Save any children you see first.'

Deliberately he cut the radio connection, and Oliver stared wordlessly at him for a second, then straightened up.

'I…I have to go,' he said with difficulty. 'Chloe…she's in Fisherman's Row.'

'You're going nowhere,' Tom declared, swinging round in his seat, as Oliver made for the office door. 'Number one, you'll never get across the Lanson, and, number two, we need you here.'

'Chloe needs me more,' Oliver said tightly, and Tom shook his head, his face impassive.

'No, she doesn't,' he said. 'If she's not in the house, she's safe. If she *is* in the house, the only people who will be able to rescue her are the helicopter winch men.'

'But you said they were to rescue children first. Chloe—'

'You put me in charge,' Tom declared, his voice level, flat, 'and you said you would accept whatever decision I made. My decision is they lift any children they see first, and you are to stay here. It's a question of priorities, Oliver.'

'A lifeboat, then,' Oliver said, dragging his fingers through his hair in desperation as, overhead, they all heard the drum of helicopter blades. 'Can't you at least ask them to launch the lifeboat?'

'Oliver, the water's running too fast for a lifeboat to make any kind of headway,' Tom protested, 'and I can't—I won't—order men to put their lives at risk for one woman.'

'I notice you're not out there endangering yourself with the men you profess to care so much about.' Oliver flared. 'You're sitting in here, all nice and warm and comfortable.'

A flash of anger appeared on Tom's face and when he got to his feet Eve instantly moved between the two men.

'Oliver—Tom—please,' she protested, but neither were listening to her.

'If I were a pilot, I'd be up there, doing my damnedest to save people,' Tom said with difficulty, 'but I'm not a pilot. When the water ebbs I'll be out there with my men, but until then I'm doing what you asked me to do—co-ordinating, and organising this operation.'

'And that's all this is to you, isn't it, just another operation?' Oliver said, fury and fear mixed on his face. 'You don't give a damn about Chloe. To you, she isn't even a person, she's just a statistic, a nameless, faceless nobody.'

'Oliver…' Tom's mouth compressed for a second, and when he eventually spoke his voice was strained. 'Believe me, this is as hard for me as it is for you, but I have to prioritise.'

'And if Chloe dies?' Oliver exclaimed, and Eve saw Tom's eyes darken.

'I'm sorry, Oliver.'

'Sorry?' Oliver echoed in anguish. 'You're *sorry*? How do you live with yourself, Cornish—how do you sleep nights?'

'I live with myself because making hard decisions is what I'm paid for, and as for sleeping…' Tom's lips curved into a bitter parody of a smile. 'I actually sleep very badly, if you want the God's honest truth, but I'm still not ordering the lifeboat to put to sea, and I want you to go back into the hall and see if there are any people needing your medical services.'

For a moment Oliver looked as though he intended to argue, then his jaw set and he strode out of the small office, banging the door behind him, and Eve turned awkwardly to Tom.

'Tom, what Oliver said… He didn't mean it, not really.'

'I know,' he murmured, sitting down again, and turning his attention back to the radio. 'But there honestly isn't anything I can do but hope Chloe either isn't in the house, or when the water started to come in she had the sense to head for the attic.'

He sounded drained. Completely, and utterly drained, and for a moment she hesitated then walked up behind him and put her arms round him.

'It's hard to believe, isn't it,' she said, 'that a little over an hour ago we were walking up the street, discussing where we would have lunch, and you said not the Anchor Hotel because you felt they always suspected you of stealing their cutlery?'

He gave a husky chuckle.

'Yeah, well, this afternoon's the day they stopped needing to worry about their cutlery.'

She gazed out of the office window, seeing nothing but darkness illuminated by the strobe lights of a hovering helicopter.

'Is it always like this, Tom? The rescue missions you and your men go out on. Are they always like this?'

'Pretty much,' he replied and, as she held him tighter, she felt his head fall back against her chest.

'How do you stand it?' she said. 'How can you bear it?'

'Because I have to,' he said quietly. 'It's my job, what I signed up for, what I agreed to do. I know Oliver thinks I'm a completely unfeeling bastard, but children always come first in a disaster, and to launch the lifeboat, risk the lives of eight— ten—men in conditions I know would be suicide...'

'Tom...'

She didn't get a chance to say any more. The office door opened and, when Chief Constable Lachlan D'Ancey appeared, she stepped away from Tom quickly.

'I picked up the emergency message on my car radio,' the policeman gasped, pulling off his cap and sending rain drops scattering everywhere, 'so I knew it was going to be bad, but I never thought it would be as bad as this. I've got men out sand-bagging Harbour Road, the council have brought in diggers, but nothing is stopping it from spreading.'

'Have you closed the roads into Penhally?' Tom asked. 'The last thing we want is people returning from work, adding to the chaos.'

'We've blockaded all the roads, and I can tell you it's holy murder out there. The word's already gone out that Penhally's in a bad way, and husbands—wives—are trying to get back into the village to find their loved ones. Luckily, a lot of the stay-at-home mums, and the elderly, seem to have taken police advice and made their way towards either Smugglers' or here, but we've no way of knowing just how many people are out there, trapped.'

'Lauren's just rung in,' Hazel declared as she appeared behind Chief Constable D'Ancey. 'She made it to Gow Court, and she's now going to try to make her way to the school hall.'

'Any word from Dragan?' Eve asked, and the practice manager shook her head.

'I'm guessing he's still out of range, and it's taking him a little while to get to The Smugglers'.'

But surely not this long, Eve thought, but she didn't say it and neither, she noticed, did Tom.

'I'd better get back outside,' Chief Constable D'Ancey declared, 'see what's happening.' His eyes met Tom's. 'Any orders—instructions—advice?'

'How about praying it stops raining?' Tom replied as another deluge began to bounce off the school roof, and the policeman smiled wryly.

'I doubt if I have a direct line to the Big Man upstairs, but I'll do my best.'

He didn't linger, and when he had gone, Hazel turned to Eve apologetically.

'Could you have a word with Lizzie Chamberlain? I've told her time and time again that Harbour View is probably the safest place in Penhally for her mother to be at the moment, but she's stressing like crazy.'

Eve glanced across at Tom enquiringly, and he nodded.

'Take a break—you deserve one,' he said, and Hazel rolled her eyes as she led the way out of the office.

'I don't think anyone could call this a break,' she muttered. 'Lizzie is a wonderful woman, and I admire her no end for all the work she does with abandoned animals but if her BP isn't through the roof mine certainly is after listening to her for the last half-hour.'

Eve chuckled, but it didn't take her long to discover that the practice manager wasn't exaggerating. Lizzie had worked herself into a complete panic attack, and eventually Eve had to concede defeat and call Oliver over to give her a sedative.

'I very much doubt she'll be the only one who cracks tonight,' Oliver declared, his face tight, strained. 'Look around you, Eve, see how crowded the place is, and yet there's scarcely a sound.'

The young doctor was right. Everywhere Eve looked she could see people sitting either in silent huddles, white-faced with shock, holding onto their families, or sitting alone, and those who were sitting alone watched the school-hall door constantly, clearly desperately hoping the next person who came in would be one of their loved ones.

'Eve…'

She knew what Oliver was going to say, just as she also knew she had no words of comfort to give him, but she was saved from saying anything when a familiar figure appeared beside her.

'Amanda, I'm so pleased to see you,' she said, turning towards Tassie's mother with relief. 'I was hoping you and your family would come here. Is there anything you need—anything I can get you?'

'We're fine, Eve,' Mrs Lovelace replied. 'A nice policeman told us to bring some food with us so we're not going to starve, but…' She glanced in the direction of her family. 'Do you think we'll have to stay long? My boys are getting a bit restless.'

They would, Eve thought as she stared at Amanda's children. The woman's three sons were looking as truculent and surly as ever, while Kelly, Amanda's eldest daughter, appeared to be painting her fingernails with an air of unutterable boredom.

'Where's Tassie?' she asked.

'Tassie?' Amanda repeated. 'But, I thought… I mean, isn't she with you?'

'No, she's not with me,' Eve said, seeing a flash of fear cross the woman's face, and knowing her own face had just mirrored it. 'Wasn't she at school today?'

'She said she didn't feel well—'

'Skiving, more like,' Tassie's twin brother Terry muttered sullenly, but his mother ignored him.

'She said she felt a bit better after lunch, and when she asked if she could go for a walk I thought she meant she was coming down to see you.'

'No, she didn't come to see me,' Eve said, fighting to stay calm, but knowing she was losing the battle. 'Have you talked to any of her friends—asked if they've seen her?'

'Nobody's seen her, Eve,' Amanda protested, panic plain now in her voice. 'You don't think—? You know how she liked to borrow books from Miss Stanbury—you don't think she could have gone to…to Gull Close?'

Please, God, no, Eve thought, as she stared wordlessly at Tassie's mother. Please, God, don't let Tassie be there, not there, and blindly she turned and hurried towards the office, her heart hammering.

'Tom—'

He held up his hand to silence her as she rushed in.

'OK, Mitch,' he said. 'Can you give me an update when you're closer to Stephanie Richards's house?'

'Will do,' the pilot replied. 'OAO.'

'Tom, Amanda doesn't know where Tassie is,' Eve said before he'd even hit the cut button on his handset. 'She wasn't at school today—she didn't feel well—but she went for a walk after lunch, and no one's seen her since.'

'And?' he said, getting stiffly to his feet.

'You have to find her,' she declared, wondering why he was suddenly being so unnecessarily dense. 'She must be out there somewhere so you have to find her.'

'The chopper pilots are picking up everyone who looks as though they're in trouble so hopefully they'll see her.'

'And that's *it*?' she protested, her voice rising despite her best efforts to prevent it. 'That's all you're going to do—*hope* Tassie is seen by somebody? Tom, she's just a little girl, just ten years old, and if she's trapped somewhere she's going to be terrified out of her mind.'

'As will be a lot of people at the moment,' he murmured, and

she grabbed hold of the front of his sweater, knowing she undoubtedly looked wild-eyed and deranged but she didn't care.

'Please, Tom, you have to do something. Get your friend—
Mad Mitch—back on the radio, tell him what Tassie looks
like—'

'For God's sake, Eve, the only lights out there are the helicopter search lights,' Tom flared. 'The pilots will scour all the
rooftops, but I can't—and won't—order them to look for one
specific child. While they're doing that, other men, women and
children could drown.'

'*I don't care!*' Eve cried, then took an unsteady breath when
Tom stared at her in shocked astonishment. 'I'm sorry—I don't
mean that—not really, but this is Tassie, Tom. *Tassie.*'

'Eve—'

'Tom—if you're there, mate, we have a problem.'

Tom eased Eve's fingers from his sweater and picked up the
handset.

'What's wrong, Mitch?'

'I'm over Bridge Street, and can see the white pillowcase
you mentioned for the woman who's giving birth, but, Tom, I
can't take a woman in labour out of that small window. When
the baby's arrived, we can do a scoop and run, but a woman in
labour, over that water, I'm sorry, but I can't.'

'I understand,' Tom said. 'Mitch—'

'I have to go, mate. I can see a couple of kids—one about
two, the other about three—sitting with a woman astride one
of the roofs in Bridge Street, and there's a blonde-haired girl of
about nine hanging out of an attic window in Gull Close.'

'*Tassie,*' Eve breathed. 'Tom, that'll be Tassie. Tell him to
pick her up first—please tell him to pick her up first.'

Tom gazed at her for a long moment, then hit the 'talk'
button on his handset.

'Pick up the youngsters on the roof and their mother first,
Mitch.'

'*No!*' Eve exclaimed. 'Tom—'

'The child hanging out of a window in Gull Close is safe for the moment, Eve,' he replied, 'but those kids on the roof have no shelter, no protection. If one of them slips—'

'But—'

'It's a question of priorities, Eve.'

'You keep saying that,' she said, feeling tears begin to trickle down her cheeks, and she rubbed them away roughly with the back of her hand. 'Like…like it's some sort of justification.'

He caught her by the shoulders, his face dark, and forced her to look up at him.

'It's the only justification I have, Eve. Can't you see that?'

'Then I'll go and help her,' she said blindly. 'If you can't—won't—I have to. I'm not going to let her down. I'm not going to abandon her the way I—' She bit off the rest of what she'd been about to say. 'She's a little girl, Tom, just a little girl, out there in the dark, and she must be terrified.'

'Eve, you are not leaving this hall.'

'I have to—don't you see that?' she cried. 'I can't live with another twenty years of regret, spend another twenty years wishing I'd done things differently.'

'Eve, you're talking nonsense,' Tom declared, giving her shoulders a little shake. 'You have never let anybody down in your life.'

'But I have, I have,' she insisted, knowing she was crying in earnest now, that her words were coming out choked with sobs. 'And I won't do that again. I *can't,* Tom.'

'Eve, you're not making any sense. Who did you let down?'

She could see the complete bewilderment in his face, and she didn't want to tell him. She'd always sworn she never would, but if she told him maybe he'd understand, maybe he would send people to help Tassic, and she took a ragged breath.

'Our baby, Tom. I let our baby down.'

He stared at her blankly.

'Eve, we don't have a baby. Look, shock can play strange tricks, affect people differently. I'll get Oliver—'

'Listen to me, Tom,' she interrupted, clutching hold of him, 'you have to listen to me. I didn't realise I was pregnant until a month after you left for America. I hadn't been feeling well, and I thought it was simply something I'd eaten until I was talking to one of the midwives at the practice I was working at in Newquay, and the penny dropped.'

'But…' He shook his head. 'You can't have been pregnant. You were on the Pill. You told me so.'

'Maybe it took longer to begin working on me—maybe it just didn't work properly—I don't know,' she protested. 'But I took one of the pregnancy kits from the surgery I was working in, and when it came up positive I thought it was a mistake— was so sure it must be a mistake—that I went up to Truro and bought another one, and…'

'It came up positive, too?'

She nodded. 'I was pregnant, Tom.'

'And you had a miscarriage,' Tom said, grasping both of her hands tightly in his. 'Oh, hell, Eve, if I'd only known, had been there with you.'

'I didn't have a miscarriage, Tom.'

'You mean…' His eyes searched hers, and she saw amazement followed by dawning delight appear in them. 'You mean, I have a son or a daughter? Eve, that is—'

'You don't have a son or a daughter, Tom,' she interrupted, her voice uneven. 'I…I had an abortion.'

# CHAPTER FIVE

HE DIDN'T believe her. She could see the disbelief and denial in his face, knew he was expecting her to suddenly smile and say, 'I didn't mean that,' but as she continued to stare silently back at him, she saw his incredulous expression gradually turn into one of shocked horror.

'You had an abortion?' he said hoarsely. 'You aborted our child?'

'I didn't want to do it, Tom,' she said, returning the pressure of his fingers, willing him to believe her. 'If there had been any other way—if I could somehow have kept the baby—but I couldn't, and believe me there hasn't been a day since then when I haven't regretted what I did.'

'You had an abortion,' he repeated as though by saying it he could somehow make it untrue.

'Yes,' she whispered, and he let go of her hands, and stepped back from her, revulsion flooding his face.

'How *could* you have done that?' he demanded. 'How *could* you have taken the life of an innocent child and just thrown it away?'

His words and his expression cut her to the bone but, as she stared back at him, saw the disgust in his eyes, it wasn't pain she felt, it was anger. A blind, furious anger that he could judge her so easily, and so instantly.

'You think,' she said, her voice shaking so much she could hardly get the words out, 'you think I just did the test, and thought, Oh, good heavens, I'm pregnant, now that's really inconvenient, but never mind, I'll *get rid of it*?'

'I don't know what you thought,' he threw back at her. 'How can I when I don't feel like I know you at all? All these years and you said nothing. All these years when I could have had a son or a daughter, but you chose to go ahead…to…without telling me… It was my child, too, Eve.'

'A child you wouldn't have wanted—not then,' she cried, her heart thumping so hard she was sure he must hear it. 'Time and time again, that summer, you told me you didn't want to be tied down, didn't want a wife, or a family, wanted to be free, to make something of your life.'

'You didn't give me the chance to say whether I wanted our baby or not,' he declared, his face twisted with fury and anguish. 'You just decided, without a word, a call…'

'*How* could I have contacted you, Tom?' she protested. '"I'm off to the States," you said, and then I got a postcard from New York, and another one from California saying you were applying for a job with Deltaron, but you never even bothered to tell me whether you'd got the job. All I knew—guessed—was you were somewhere in America. Well, America is a pretty big place, Tom.'

'You…you could have phoned the offices of Deltaron,' he said defensively. 'They would have told you where I was.'

'And if I'd done that—turned up on your doorstep—and said, "I'm pregnant, Tom," how would you have felt?' she demanded. 'What would you have done?'

'I would…I could have offered to help,' he said, beginning to pace backwards and forwards across the small office, his face a tight mask of anger, his green eyes blazing. 'OK, so maybe I wasn't making very much money then, but I could have sent you something every month to help you take care of the baby.'

'And resented me and the child for the rest of our lives for putting you in that position.'

He whirled round at her, his face so contorted that she involuntarily took a step back.

'How *dare* you say that?' he exclaimed. 'I would *never* have resented my child. You know how I feel about children.'

'I know how you feel now,' she countered, bunching her hands into tight fists at her sides, 'but that wasn't how you felt when we were young.'

'Eve—'

'You wanted freedom. "No emotional baggage", that's what you said you wanted, and if I'd told you about the baby… Do you think I wanted you to hate him or her as much as your father hated and resented you?'

'So, it's my fault, now, is it?' he flared.

'Tom—'

'Eve Oliver—is anyone there?'

Dragan's voice crackled over the radio, insistent, concerned, and when Tom made no move to answer it Eve shakily lifted the handset, and hit the reply button.

'I…I hear you, Dragan,' she said with difficulty. 'Where are you?'

'The Smugglers' Inn, as per instructions. I gather things are pretty bad in Penhally?'

Eve glanced across at Tom's rigid back.

'You could say that,' she replied.

'Well, I'm sorry to add to your troubles, but I need a helicopter asap,' Dragan continued. 'Tony, at the Smugglers', has apparently been experiencing chest pains for the past month, but he's been ignoring them, thinking they were due to indigestion, but the pain's so bad even he can't ignore it. Chloe says—'

'Chloe's there?' Eve interrupted quickly.

'She was visiting Rachel Kenner at the manse when the word to evacuate went out, so she and Rachel came here. Why?'

'She hasn't had her mobile switched on, and Oliver's been a bit worried about her,' she said. *Which had to be the biggest understatement of the year.* 'You think Tony's having a heart attack?'

'His BP's 130 over 90, his skin's sweaty, and the pain's radiating from his chest down his left arm and up into his jaw, so I think we can safely say he's having a heart attack,' Dragan replied. 'I've given him nitro to relieve the pain, and Chloe's started an IV line of morphine, but he needs hospital, Eve, and fast.'

Out of the corner of her eye, Eve could see Tom holding out his hand for the handset, and she gave it to him.

'I'll get one of the Navy guys to Smugglers' Inn right away, Dragan,' he declared. 'Could somebody put out a light, or a flare, to show the chopper where you are?'

There was a distant murmur of conversation from Dragan's side of the connection, and then Dragan's voice rang out.

'We're on it, Tom, but can you be quick? Tony's not in good shape.'

Tom handed the handset back to Eve, then picked up their spare.

'Keep him on the radio,' he said abruptly. 'I can page the Navy with this, and then give him an ETA.'

Eve nodded.

'Is Melinda all right, Dragan?' she said, turning back to the radio.

'Would you believe she's actually watching what's happening in Penhally on television?' the Croatian doctor replied. 'She said she couldn't believe it when part of The Anchor collapsed.'

'Someone's been filming this?' Eve gasped, and heard the Croatian doctor give a wry chuckle.

'Eve, people would film a car crash if they thought they could make a quick buck out of it.'

'Tell him the ETA for the helicopter is five minutes,' Tom declared.

'No need to tell me,' Dragan said. 'I heard it myself. Thanks, Tom, and now I'd better go,' he added. 'There's quite a crowd gathering here, and some of them are panicking pretty badly.'

'Tell Melinda to stay where she is when you next talk to her,' Eve said. 'And tell her not to do anything stupid, like going out to check her animals.'

'I've already told her that,' Dragan replied. 'Got an earful back for my pains, of course, but when I first heard about what was happening in Penhally, all I could think was, Please, God, don't let her be there. Just the thought of losing her, and the baby…'

'I know,' Eve said softly, and heard Tom draw in a ragged breath behind her, but she didn't turn round, couldn't. 'Call us if there's anything else you need, OK?'

She heard Dragan's muttered assent but, after she'd switched off the reply button, she stared at the radio equipment for a long moment before she hesitantly turned towards Tom.

'That's good news,' she said. 'About Chloe, I mean.'

He nodded, but he didn't meet her gaze.

'Tom…' She moistened her lips. 'Tom…'

'I'll tell Mitch to pick Tassie up next.'

'Thank you,' she said, wishing he would look at her, wishing she could touch him, but not daring to. 'Tom—'

'You'd better tell Oliver about his fiancée.'

His face was cold and forbidding, but she couldn't leave it like this—simply couldn't—and hesitantly she took a step towards him.

'Tom, about our baby,' she said, her voice choked, and he made a convulsive movement with his arm, clearly warning her not to say anything else, but she couldn't remain silent. 'Tom, you cannot possibly regret what I did more than I do.'

'You *think*?' he exclaimed, his green eyes dark, pain-filled.

'Tom… *Please*.'

The raw pain in her face tore at his heart, and part of him wanted to go to her, to hold her and comfort her, but the other part—the part inside him that hurt so much—never wanted to see her ever again.

'Just go, Eve,' he said. 'Just...*go*.'

She did. She walked stiffly out of the office, but, when she'd closed the door quietly behind her, he let his breath out in a long, shuddering gasp of pain.

How could she have done that? he wondered. She'd said she'd had no choice, but other women were single mothers, other women had brought up—were bringing up—children on their own, and for her to have...

A son. He might have had a son he could have taught how to play football, taken to matches, joked with, laughed with, advised so he wouldn't make the same mistakes he had. Or a daughter. He squeezed his eyes shut, but that didn't stop him seeing her in his mind's eye, a smaller version of Eve with big brown eyes, and a cloud of dark hair.

How could she just have gone ahead and had an abortion? He'd thought he'd known her. He'd thought in the mêlée of death and destruction that his life had become, she was the one constant, the one calm haven, and to discover she'd...

'Eve... Oh, sorry,' Hazel declared as she stuck her head round the office door. 'Where's Eve?'

'She...' Tom stared at the radio equipment, deliberately avoiding the practice manager's eye. 'She's with Oliver.'

'Oh. Right,' Hazel said. 'It's just Amanda Lovelace—she's very worried about her daughter, and she seems to be under the impression Eve knows something, or can do something.'

'Tell Mrs Lovelace we think we know where Tassie is.'

'You mean she's safe—she's been picked up?' Hazel said.

'No, she hasn't been picked up, not yet,' he replied.

'But—'

'Hazel, I'm not God,' he snapped, then held up his hands

apologetically when the practice manager blinked. 'Sorry—
I…I'm sorry.'

'It's OK,' Hazel said, her face softening with understanding.
'I'll be as encouraging as I can to Amanda, without being too
specific.'

He nodded but, when the practice manager had disappeared,
he bit down hard on his lip to quell the sob he could feel welling
in his throat.

To think he'd told Eve just a few short hours ago that one of
the reasons he'd come back to Penhally had been to see if he
could still feel anything. Well, by God, he knew he could. He
was caring so much right now he felt as though he would die of
it, and, desperately, he glanced around the silent office, searching for some way to release the anger and despair he felt, but
there was no way, and he knew there wasn't. Nothing could ease
what he felt inside. Nothing could remove the knowledge that
he could have had a son, or a daughter, and that Eve had taken
that from him. Taken it without asking him, or even telling him
what she'd done.

How could she have told you? a small voice whispered at
the back of his mind, but he didn't listen to it, didn't want to.
All he wanted was the pain to go away, for him never to have
known, because the knowledge was tearing him apart.

'Eve, are you there?'

Tom swore as Nick's voice rang out on the radio. The senior
partner was the last person he wanted to talk to right now, but
he couldn't ignore the voice.

'It's me, Nick,' he said, flicking on the handset.

'Oh. Right.'

Nick's clipped tone said it all, and a horrible suspicion
suddenly crept into Tom's mind. Could Eve had gone to Nick,
all those years ago, asked him to authorise her request for a termination, and that was why Nick always looked at him as
though he was something unmentionable stuck to the bottom

of his shoe? It would have made more sense for her to have gone outside the area, to a doctor she didn't know, but, then, he didn't know anything with any certainty any more.

'St Piran's?'

Tom stared blankly at the radio equipment. Nick had clearly asked him something, but he hadn't been listening.

'Sorry, Nick, interference on the line,' Tom lied. 'Can you say that again?'

'I said,' Nick declared with clear impatience, 'that Stephanie's just given birth to a boy, and she really needs to be in hospital so we'd appreciate the appearance of a helicopter as quickly as possible.'

Despite everything, Tom could not prevent a wry smile from curving his lips at the senior partner's peremptory tone. When Nick said, 'Jump', he clearly expected people to obey irrespective of the circumstances.

'You're a priority two, Nick, if that's any consolation,' he said, then hit the talk button so he could speak to Mitch.

'Did you hear that?' Nick said, turning to Kate as he put down his handset. 'We're a priority two.'

'Good to know we're somewhere on the list,' Kate said with a wobbly smile, 'especially as our torches aren't going to last much longer.'

Nick nodded, then frowned.

'I feel so damned useless, stuck in here,' he protested. 'All my patients are out there, and I'm trapped in here and about as much use as a chocolate fireguard.'

'Stephanie Richards didn't think you were useless,' Kate pointed out. 'A breech birth isn't easy to pull off even with every surgical piece of equipment known to mankind, but you did it with just what was in your bag.'

Nick shook his head. 'Flattery will get you nowhere.'

'Not flattery,' she said. 'You're a good doctor, Nick, you

always were, and…' She came to a halt as the building swayed slightly. 'I wish it wouldn't do that.'

'Stop fretting,' Nick replied. 'This building's made of good Cornish stone. It can withstand worse than this.'

'Right,' Kate said without conviction, then flushed when Nick shook his head at her again. 'Sorry. I'm not doing positive and upbeat very well, am I? Trouble is, I'm a coward when it comes to water.' She took a shaky breath. 'Bad memories.'

'Nothing's going to happen to us, Kate,' Nick said gently, and she forced a smile.

''Course it won't.' She bent down to tuck a blanket round the young mother and her baby. 'Strange to think Stephanie was right all along. She kept saying she felt something was wrong, and I kept thinking, Here she goes again, panicking. And yet she was right.'

'I hardly think she can have known she was going to have a breech birth,' Nick observed, and Kate rolled her eyes.

'Must you be so pedantic, Nick? I didn't mean she knew she was going to have a breech birth. I just meant sometimes mums to-be have a sixth sense about whether things are right, or not.' She gazed down at the sleeping young mother. 'Actually, although she doesn't know it yet, this is when the really hard bit starts, and it's going to be doubly difficult for her as she'll have to bring up the baby on her own.'

'She'll cope,' Nick said firmly. 'It never ceases to amaze me how strong women are, and she'll cope.'

Kate nodded, and cleared her throat.

'Do you think Jem's all right?'

Nick's eyes met hers, calm, unreadable.

'I should imagine they've kept all the kids in school,' he said, 'and, as both the high school and the primary school are up on a hill, he'll be fine.'

'Yes,' Kate said, more in an attempt to convince herself than in actual agreement. 'It's just he's like me—not keen on water.'

'Nothing's going to happen to him, Kate.'

'No, of course not,' she said with an effort. 'Do you think it will be Tom who will come with the helicopter?'

'God, I hope not.' Nick groaned. 'That would be all I'd need. The mighty Tom Cornish winching me out of a window.'

Kate tilted her head, and gazed at him speculatively. 'You seriously dislike him, don't you?'

'Yes.'

'Care to share the reason?'

'Can't,' Nick said tightly. 'Patient confidentiality.'

'It's got something to do with Eve Dwyer, hasn't it?' Kate pressed. 'She looked as though she'd seen a ghost when he turned up at Alison and Jack's wedding.'

'Kate—'

'Nick, given that we're both medical professionals, and we could well be dependent on Tom to rescue us,' Kate exclaimed, 'don't you think I have the right to know what he did that has made you dislike him so much?'

For a second she saw indecision warring with professionalism on Nick's face, then he sighed.

'Eve came to me twenty years ago, asking for a prescription for antibiotics. She told me she had a vaginal infection. Well, there was no way I was going to prescribe anything without examining her first, so I did. She'd had an abortion, Eve.'

'And you think Tom was the father?' Kate said calmly.

'Kate, it was common knowledge twenty years ago that they were lovers.'

'You mean it was Penhally gossip, twenty years ago,' Kate replied dryly, and Nick looked irritated.

'She wasn't going out with anyone else at the time, so I think we can safely say he fathered her baby. And what did he do? He skipped off to the US, leaving Eve to deal with it.'

'He might not have known she was pregnant when he left,' Kate protested. 'He might only have found out later.'

'He didn't come back, though, did he?' Nick countered. 'And what kind of man does that?'

'Nick—'

'Kate, I was just nineteen when Annabel and I got married, and I was a father to twins soon after. I don't know how Annabel and I survived those early years, never knowing where the next meal was coming from, always panic-stricken that we wouldn't be able to pay the rent, but I would never have suggested she have an abortion.'

'Nick…' Gently, Kate put her hand on his arm. 'Things are seldom black and white, right or wrong, and who are we to judge? Our haloes are hardly shiny bright. Ten years ago—'

'I don't want to talk about this,' Nick interrupted, throwing her hand off, and walking towards the window, but Kate followed him.

'Nick, we might die tonight,' she said, 'and I don't want to die with what I need to say to you—what I've wanted to say to you for the past ten years—left unsaid.'

His face contorted, and for a second she thought he was going to refuse to listen to her, then his shoulders slumped.

'Do you have any idea how much I deeply regret that night?' he said hoarsely as he stared out of the window into the blackness. 'It should never have happened, and I blame myself entirely.'

'Nick, it takes two to make love, and I didn't push you away,' Kate said softly. 'I could have done—should have done—and yet I didn't. I wanted you that night as much as you wanted me, and when I heard James had died…' She closed her eyes, then opened them again. 'I knew it was a punishment. That God had taken my husband from me to punish me.'

'Oh, Kate…'

'No, please, let me finish,' she insisted as he turned towards her, his face taut. 'We made love that night. You were unfaithful to your wife, and I was unfaithful to my husband, and it was wrong—so very wrong—and when I discovered I was pregnant…'

'Are you telling me you actually considered having an abortion?' Nick said, horror plain in his voice, and tears appeared in Kate's eyes.

'Maybe I should have done. It would certainly have made everything easier for us both, wouldn't it, with no living reminder of what we'd done, but despite all the guilt I've felt over the years, all the torment…' Kate's voice broke. 'As God is my witness, even though I know I will be damned for all eternity for saying this, I can't—and won't ever—regret having him.'

Nick reached out and jerkily clasped her hands in his.

'Kate, if there is a God, he would never condemn you, but what I can't forgive myself for—will never be able to forgive myself for—is cheating on Annabel that night, betraying my marriage vows.'

'And you think I can forgive myself for betraying James?' Kate demanded. 'You think I'm saying that because Jem has brought me so much happiness, his birth justified what we did? I'm not saying that, Nick, I would never say that, but…'

'But?' he prompted, and she could see the uncertainty in his eyes, and the pain.

'We can't undo it, Nick. We will both have to live with our guilt until the day we die, and if by some miracle we're spared tonight then what I want—what I hope—is for us both to perhaps be able to move on, move forward. Not forgetting what we did— we won't ever be able to—but living with it, accepting it, and for you—maybe in time—to let Jem become a part of your life.'

'Kate…'

His voice was deep, strained, but she didn't get a chance to find out what he'd been about to say. A light suddenly appeared at the window, followed by the sound of a gloved hand knocking against it.

'You have a woman and a newborn in here?' the winch man asked when Nick opened the window, and, when Nick nodded, the winch man grinned. 'Then your helicopter awaits, and Tom Cornish sends his compliments.'

'He would,' Nick said darkly.

'And Chloe really is safe?' Oliver declared for what felt, to Eve, like the hundredth time, and she nodded.

'Yes, she really is safe,' she said.

'No thanks to Tom,' the young doctor muttered as he gazed out over the crowded school hall, then flushed when he saw Eve's expression. 'I'm sorry, but he didn't exactly help, did he?'

'Oliver, it's not his fault only one helicopter can fly into Penhally at a time because the entrance to the harbour is so narrow,' she protested. 'It's not his fault the water's rushing so high and fast it would be suicide to launch a boat. What else could he have done—what would you have done if you'd been in his shoes?'

'Saved the woman I loved first,' he said simply, and Eve managed a smile.

'Which is why neither you nor I would make very good heads of operations at Deltaron,' she said. 'We can't see the bigger picture.'

'I'd rather keep my ability to feel, to care,' Oliver declared, and, as Eve caught sight of Tom coming out of the small office, her smile died.

'Tom has the ability to feel, Oliver,' she murmured, 'and to care, very deeply.'

And to hate, she thought, feeling her heart contract as Tom's gaze stopped momentarily on her without expression, then moved away.

'Eve?'

Oliver looked concerned, puzzled, and she forced her smile back into place.

'How's everyone doing?' she said.

'Those who have their families with them are obviously coping better than the others.'

'Are…?' Eve swallowed hard. 'Are there many missing?'

'We don't know,' Oliver admitted. 'What with half the village being here, the other half at The Smugglers', and some people away at work… Chief Constable D'Ancey has put the number missing at around eighteen, but that's purely guesswork.'

'*Eighteen?*' Eve echoed in horror, and Oliver squeezed her hand.

'It's guesswork only, Eve. We'll know better when it's daylight, when the water starts to go down. Hopefully, nobody is lost at all, and people are just sheltering where they can.'

'Lizzie Chamberlain's looking a little better,' she observed, and Oliver nodded.

'She should do, considering the size of sedative I gave her. Amanda Lovelace is understandably in a bit of a state, but she point blank refuses to let me give her anything.'

And Tom was talking to her, Eve noticed. He was bending down towards Tassie's mother, then suddenly she saw Amanda's face light up, and she was gripping his hand tightly, and he was shaking his head, his cheeks darkening slightly, at whatever she'd said.

Could this mean Tassie was on her way? She prayed the girl was. She prayed, too, that Gertrude Stanbury had survived. The elderly school teacher was a determined, spunky woman, but she was crippled with arthritis, and though Tassie was agile enough to have reached the attic she couldn't see how Gertrude could possibly have managed to clamber up there.

'Is…is Tassie safe?' Eve said hesitantly as Tom passed her, and he paused; but he didn't look at her.

'Mitch has picked both her and Gertie Stanbury up. He's going to drop them on the playing fields, and the police will bring them here.'

Eve closed her eyes tightly.

'Thank you,' she whispered. 'Thank you.'

'Nick knows, doesn't he?'

Eve's eyes flew open. 'What?'

Tom caught her by the arm, and steered her none too gently back into the school office.

'Nick—you went to Nick, didn't you, when you decided you weren't going to have the baby?'

'No— I— No,' she faltered. 'I went up to Bude when I discovered I was pregnant. I had…I had it done there.'

'But Nick knows.'

Tom's face was tight with barely suppressed anger, and she wished she could lie, but there was no point.

'He knows I had an abortion,' she said. 'I didn't realise until quite recently that he knew—had guessed—but I caught an infection afterwards, so I had to go to him for antibiotics and he must have guessed then.'

'Which is why he thinks I'm scum,' Tom said. 'He thinks I walked out on you when you were pregnant, forced you into having the abortion.'

'Why would he think that?' she protested. 'Why would he even suspect you were the father?'

'Oh, give me credit for some intelligence,' Tom said, his voice harsh, bitter. 'You and I were an item that summer so he had to suspect it was me, didn't he?'

'Tom—'

'What else haven't you told me?' he said, talking right over her. 'What else don't I know?'

'You know everything now,' she said wretchedly. 'You're the only one who does. No one else. I told no one else.'

'Couldn't your parents have helped?' he demanded. 'I know they didn't have much money, but—'

'They didn't know either.'

He stared at her blankly.

'They didn't know? But—'

'Tom, you know what my parents were like,' she cried. 'My dad—he was a kind man, a generous man, but he disapproved of me even going out with you. He would have said I'd made my bed, and I had to lie in it, and my mum… She would have wanted to help, but this was twenty years ago, and her first thought would have been, What will the neighbours say?'

'So, you kept this from them,' he said, 'just as you kept it from me.'

'And I paid for it, Tom,' she said, her voice thick with unshed tears. 'Because I couldn't tell them, because they never knew they could have been grandparents, it got harder and harder for me to face them so I visited them less and less, so I lost my parents, too. I didn't just lose my baby, I lost my parents, too.'

'But you didn't have to,' he protested. 'Even twenty years ago, women had babies without being married, without their parents' approval.'

'Tom, I'd only just qualified as a nurse, and you know what the wages were like back then,' she said, willing him to understand. 'I thought of adoption, but what was I going to live on while I was pregnant, unable to work? I was twenty-two, Tom, and I was scared witless. I couldn't see any other way out.'

'If you didn't want it—'

'Don't…don't you *dare* say that to me,' she said, her voice breaking on a sob. 'Don't you *dare* say I didn't want my baby. I would have given anything to have kept that baby.'

'Except given birth to it.'

'I *loved* you, Tom,' she replied, feeling her heart splinter with absolute loneliness at the coldness in his voice. 'I loved you back in school even when you and your friends used to shout "Starchy Dwyer" after me in the corridor. And when I discovered I was pregnant, knew there was a part of you growing inside me, I wanted to keep your baby so badly, but I couldn't—I *couldn't*.'

'So you just…you just…'

'Took the easy way out,' she finished for him. 'That's what you're accusing me of, isn't it, taking the easy way out?'

'Perhaps not the easy way out,' he muttered, hot colour darkening his cheeks. 'Maybe that was the wrong thing to say.'

'You want to know how easy it is to have an abortion, Tom?' she said, her voice every bit as hard as his now. 'Then maybe I should tell you. Maybe I should tell you *exactly* how easy it is to have an abortion.'

'I know what the procedure involves,' he said, turning his back on her, and she came after him, and grabbed his arm.

'Maybe you do—medically,' she said, forcing him round to face her. 'But you don't know what it's like emotionally. You don't know what it's like to sit in a waiting room full of women where nobody makes eye contact, and nobody talks, because you all know why you're there, and you're all locked inside your own private little hell.'

'Eve, I don't want to hear this,' he said, pulling his arm free and walking away from her, but she followed him.

'And the nurses,' she continued, 'maybe it was my imagination, but I felt—I thought—that all I could see in their eyes were the unspoken words, "You should have known better. You should have been sensible, should have used a condom, or been on the Pill," and I wanted to yell at them that I had been on the Pill, that this wasn't supposed to have happened, but I didn't say anything because I knew…' Her lips trembled. 'I knew if I started yelling I would never stop.'

He turned to face her, his face white, taut. 'Look, if I've implied—'

'And all the time you're sitting in the waiting room you're thinking, you're thinking…' She choked down a sob. 'That you can still change your mind, you don't have to go through with this, you can still change my mind, but you know you won't because you've been through all the options in your head a thousand times, and you know there isn't anything else you can do.'

'Eve—please—I don't want to hear any more,' he said, his voice cold.

He clearly didn't, she realised as she met his gaze and saw no sympathy or compassion at all in his green eyes, only complete condemnation, and, as tears began to trickle down her cheeks, she felt as empty and as utterly alone as she had felt all those years ago.

'Maybe you don't want to know, Tom, but there's one thing you should know,' she said, wiping her face with a shaking hand. 'Afterwards, when it's done, and the doctor says you can leave, they tell you it's over, but it isn't over because what you don't know—what no one tells you—is that abortion doesn't end anything. It simply starts something else.'

'I don't know what you mean,' Tom said harshly, and Eve shook her head.

'I know you don't,' she said, 'because, you see, nobody warns you that from then on you'll live a lifetime of regret. Nobody tells you you'll discover that the world is full of babies and pregnant women, and every pregnant woman you see, every…every baby you see, will remind you of what you did— what you gave up.'

'Eve—'

'And it never goes away, Tom,' she said. 'Oh, gradually, you pick up the pieces, learn somehow to go on, but it can't ever go away because there are all these dates, you see. The day when he or she would have had their first birthday, the day they would have started school, and all…' She took a ragged breath. 'All the Christmases you never share with them.'

'Eve, I—'

'You implied I took the easy way out, Tom,' she said, catching his gaze, refusing to allow him to look away. 'Well, you tell me whether you think it's been easy for me.'

He opened his mouth to reply, but, before he could say anything, Hazel had appeared, her eyes shining.

'Eve, someone's just arrived I know you'll be delighted to see,' the practice manager declared.

Quickly Eve hurried out into the school hall and when Tom followed her he saw her glance around, expectant, hopeful, and then the hall door opened, and Tassie raced in. For a second Eve's face lit up with a blinding smile but, as she held out her arms, and Tassie raced straight past her towards her mother, Tom saw her smile slide slowly sideways. Slide—just for an instant—into an expression of hurt, and then into an accepting, rueful, wistful yearning that tugged at his heart.

Tassie wasn't simply a child Eve was trying to help. Tassie was the child Eve had never had, the child she had lost.

Not lost, a small voice reminded him. Didn't want, but the small voice held no conviction. In truth, it never had. It had been his own guilt which had made him stand coldly by while Eve had poured out all her anguish and suffering. His own guilt which had kept him aloof from her, because she had been right.

He wouldn't have wanted a child when he'd been twenty-four. All the plans he'd had then, his aims, his dreams... He would have seen a child as an encumbrance, something he had been saddled with, and what kind of life would that child have had, with him rejecting her or him, giving money perhaps but even then grudgingly? He would have been his father all over again, not in the violence—never in the violence—but in the resentment, the feeling of having been cheated out of the life he had wanted, dreamt of.

Savagely, he bit his lip. How could he have accused her of taking the easy way out? She'd taken the hardest decision any woman could ever make, taken it alone, had had to live with it alone, carrying the knowledge, and the pain, for twenty years, and what had he done? He'd watched impassively as she'd broken her heart all over again in telling him. He'd been wrong—so wrong—and somehow he had to tell her that, but how could he get her to listen to him after what he had said, what he'd accused her of?

'I don't believe it,' Gertrude Stanbury declared, as she walked towards him, leaning heavily on the arm of a young policeman. 'I wondered when the pilot said he'd been sent by a Dr Cornish, but I didn't believe it really could be you, not after all these years. It's good to see you again, lad.'

'It's good to see you, too, Miss Stanbury,' he managed to reply. 'I understand you and young Tassie have had quite an afternoon.'

The old lady chuckled.

'You could say that,' she said. 'In fact, I wouldn't be here at all if it hadn't been for the girl. I told her I'd never get up into the attic—that she was to save herself—but she refused to take no for an answer, and somehow, between the two of us, she got me up there.'

'Would you like something hot to drink, Miss Stanbury?' Eve asked as she joined them. 'We've tea—coffee—cocoa…'

'Cocoa,' Miss Stanbury said firmly, 'and a seat if one's available. The young man who winched me out of my house was most kind, and reassuring, but dangling above Penhally, held only by a harness and a stranger's arms, is not my idea of a fun time out.'

Eve laughed. Gently, she and Tom helped the elderly lady across the hall, but once Eve had settled Gertrude into a seat, she straightened up and there was no laughter in her face, only an unreadable blankness.

'I expect you'll be wanting to get back to the radio, Tom,' she said.

The finality in her voice was plain and he knew, as he watched her walk away to get Gertrude cocoa, that he had been dismissed as effectively as if she'd actually closed a door on him, and he deserved it. Twice in her life he had let her down. Twice he hadn't been there for her when it had really mattered, and this last time…

'Whatever it is, lad, I'm sure you'll sort it.'

He glanced down to see Gertrude staring up at him, her small face oddly understanding, and shook his head.

'I don't think I can this time, Miss Stanbury,' he said. 'I think this time I've screwed up big time.'

# CHAPTER SIX

THE sun was shining. It was unbelievable, Eve thought as she stared up into the cloudless blue sky, but the sun was actually shining and as long as she kept looking up she could almost believe that the devastating flood which had hit Penhally yesterday had never happened. Almost, but not quite.

'I suspected it might look pretty bad this morning,' Kate murmured, 'but I never for one minute…'

The midwife's voice trailed away into silence and Eve could understand her difficulty. Yesterday Penhally had been a picture-perfect village, full of people going about their daily business, but this morning the area around the harbour looked as though some malevolent giant had taken a hammer and smashed his way through the buildings, heaping boulders, trees, telephone poles and dustbins onto roofs, and tearing up roads and pavements in his relentless march onwards.

'I'm amazed the surgery wasn't touched, or any of our homes, apart from poor Chloe and Oliver's,' Eve observed. 'They're going to stay with Lauren, aren't they, until their house can be dried out?'

'*If* it can be dried out,' Kate said dubiously. 'Tom says all the houses can be made habitable again but when you look at this…I know the Lanson's flowing within its banks again, and somehow the Harbour Bridge is still intact, but one of Tom's men told me all of the houses have at least three feet of water and mud in them.'

'I suppose Tom's the expert,' Eve said uncertainly, though she had to admit she couldn't see how anyone could ever live in Bridge Street or Gull Close again either.

'I'm just so glad Tom is here,' Kate continued. 'I wouldn't have a clue about how to begin searching for the people who are missing, would you?'

Eve shook her head as she glanced over to where Tom was deep in conversation with Nick, Chief Constable D'Ancey and a group of men dressed in coveralls emblazoned with the Deltaron insignia. It wasn't a task she would have liked and, judging by the expression on Nick's face, Tom's suggestions weren't meeting with his approval, whereas Tom...

She shifted her gaze quickly towards some of the shopkeepers who were standing in dazed huddles outside their ruined shops. She didn't know what Tom was thinking, didn't want to be anywhere near him for fear he would look at her with the same condemnation and disgust as he had done yesterday.

'How's Stephanie Richards?' she asked, deliberately changing the subject.

'She and her son are doing very well,' Kate replied, 'though goodness knows where they're going to stay when they're discharged from hospital.'

'Oliver said the owners of the Penhally Paradise Caravan Park have offered some of their caravans as temporary accommodation for people who can't go back to their homes,' Eve observed. 'And Tony has offered the use of some of the bedrooms at Smugglers' Inn.'

'Did you hear he was still giving out orders while they were carrying him out to the helicopter?' The midwife shook her head. 'The man was having a heart attack, for God's sake, and yet he was still giving out orders.'

Eve laughed. 'One of a kind, Tony.'

'So is Tom.'

Kate's gaze was fixed on her, and Eve couldn't meet the midwife's eyes.

'He's certainly a good organiser,' she said noncommittally, and Kate sighed.

'Eve, whatever happened in the past, let it go. You can't alter it—change it—so let it go.'

'What has Nick been say—?'

'This has nothing to do with Nick,' Kate interrupted as Eve's eyes shot to hers in alarm, 'this is just me talking to you, one woman to another. We've all made mistakes—me, more than most—but you have to forgive yourself your mistakes or they will simply corrode your present and your future.'

Which was easy for Kate to say, Eve thought as her gaze went back to Tom, but she couldn't forgive herself. She had learned to live with what she'd done, but she had never forgiven herself and she never would. Tom hadn't resurrected the old pain. He had simply ripped off the unhealed scab, exposing the old wound for the ugliness it was.

'Which of you two lovelies is Eve Dwyer?'

A tall man, with flaming red hair and a bushy beard, was gazing at them quizzically, and Eve managed a smile.

'I'm Eve Dwyer.'

The man's eyebrows rose.

'Do I know you?' he asked. 'Your voice sounds strangely familiar.'

She recognised his voice, too. It was Mad Mitch or, to be more accurate, Michael Flannery, the pilot from the radio last night.

'I'm the woman Tom found in the men-only changing room,' she said before she could stop herself, and the pilot threw back his head, and laughed.

'Pleased to meet you in the flesh, so to speak,' he said. 'Tom would like a word.'

'With me?' Eve said faintly.

'With you.' The pilot nodded. 'He has a suggestion to make, and your boss isn't very happy about it.'

Kate's eyes gleamed.

'Now, this I want to hear,' she said, and carefully the midwife followed Eve over the rubble-strewn pavement towards where Tom was standing.

'So, what you're basically saying is, according to your engineer, most of the shops and houses should be habitable once the water and silt have been pumped out, but the Anchor Hotel is a writeoff?' they heard Chief Constable D'Ancey declare.

'I'm afraid so,' Tom replied. 'For the moment I'd recommend you erect scaffolding to ensure no more of it comes down, but after that I'd say you're pretty well definitely looking at a demolition job.'

'When are people going to be allowed back into their homes to collect their personal possessions?' Nick demanded. 'The police can't watch every house, and people are becoming understandably twitchy about their valuables.'

'They'll become considerably twitchier if they're electrocuted,' Tom said dryly. 'The electricity company isn't sure all power has been disconnected to the village, and until they are nobody enters any house apart from me and my men.'

'Yes, but—'

'Nick, if you want to be useful, go and open up the surgery,' Tom interrupted. 'With all this polluted water lying about I should imagine you'll be inundated with people requiring tetanus injections.'

'I don't take orders—'

'I've the press at my heels wanting to come into Penhally to take photographs,' Chief Constable D'Ancey declared, cutting across Nick who shot him a fulsome look. 'They're also very keen to do an interview with you.'

'I've more important things to do than give interviews,' Tom said tightly, 'and neither do I want photographers scrambling over the rubble in search of a story. Keep them out.'

Eve saw Nick's lip curl as the chief constable hurried off to forestall the members of the press. So, too, she noticed, had Tom, and quickly she cleared her throat.

'Mitch said you had a suggestion to make to me?' she said, and Tom nodded.

'At the moment, I'm the only medic on the rescue team,' he declared. 'We have spare medi-bags but they're no use without someone who knows how to use the contents, and I wondered if you'd like to help.'

'And *I* have said,' Nick exclaimed, 'if another medic is required then Oliver or I will volunteer. Eve is not a qualified rescue worker, or a doctor.'

'But she's a fully qualified nurse, and she's small, and there may be areas that only someone small will be able to get into,' Tom said, his voice calm but with an unmistakable hint of steel beneath it. 'And I would like Eve to help, if she's willing.'

'Eve is a member of my staff, and I will not agree to this,' Nick retorted.

'I don't think it's a question of whether you agree or not,' Tom began. 'Eve—'

'Can make up her own mind, thank you very much,' she interrupted, 'so would the two of you both park your testosterone to one side for the moment, and concentrate on what's really important?'

Tom's jaw dropped, Mitch Flannery smothered a wry chuckle, and Nick looked absolutely furious, but Kate laughed.

'Well said, Eve,' she declared. 'Nick, it's Eve's decision,' she continued quickly as the senior partner opened his mouth, clearly intending to continue the argument. 'If she wants to volunteer then surely it's her choice, not yours.'

Eve didn't have the faintest idea of what she might be volunteering for but she didn't care. All that mattered to her was that Tom had specifically asked for her. She hadn't expected him to—was amazed that he had—and if he was holding out any kind of olive branch she had no intention of rejecting it.

'I want to help,' she said firmly, and saw Tom's lips curve into a hesitant smile, a smile she returned equally tentatively.

'I am Eve's boss,' Nick declared angrily, 'and I still don't think—'

'I know you don't, Nick,' Kate interrupted, 'but right now we have a surgery to open.'

And, with a backward wink at Eve, the midwife towed a clearly reluctant Nick away leaving Eve standing awkwardly beside Tom and Mitch Flannery.

'Do we know how many people we're looking for?' she asked.

'Thankfully only three people still haven't been accounted for,' Tom replied. 'Reverend Kenner, Audrey Baxter and Sophie Banks.'

'Sophie?' Eve gasped. 'But—'

'She should have been at school.' Tom nodded. 'Her mother thought she was, and so she didn't worry about her, thinking she was safe with the other kids, and the school weren't concerned because they thought Sophie had been told to take the day off after she'd been to the surgery to see you.'

'And Reverend Kenner and Audrey Baxter?' Eve said.

'A neighbour saw Mrs Baxter leaving her house just before the river broke its banks,' Mitch Flannery declared. 'Reverend Kenner appeared to be trying to persuade her to go back into her house but, since then, there's been no sign of either of them.'

'Mitch, do we have any protective coveralls and thermals that would fit Eve?' Tom said, his gaze taking in her jeans, sweater and sturdy boots.

'I doubt we've anything small enough,' the pilot said dubiously. 'Gregory's our shortest man, but even he's a good four inches taller than this lass.'

Gregory was.

'If you laugh at me, you're a dead man,' Eve warned a little later, when Mitch led her back to Tom and she saw his lips twitch as his gaze took in her rolled-up sleeves and trouser legs.

'Would I laugh?' he protested, and she nodded.

'Without a second's thought,' she said, and heard Mitch guffaw.

'Keeper, Tom,' the pilot observed. 'Trust me, this one's a keeper.'

'A keeper of what?' Eve said in confusion but, for an answer, Tom placed a string round her neck with a whistle at the end.

'Blow once on this if you spot somebody alive, and blow twice if you see a body. It's standard rescue procedure,' he continued as she stared down at the whistle.

'Right,' she said, swallowing hard, and praying she would only have to blow once on the whistle as Tom called for his men's attention.

'Does everyone have a thermal imaging camera?' he asked and, when his question was greeted with a series of nods, he added, 'OK, Mitch, I want you and your men to survey Bridge Street. Gregory, you and your team will do Gull Close, Frank, you take Harbour Road. I'll do Fisherman's Row, and if anyone spots any signs of life, it's the usual drill.'

Obediently, the men split themselves into four groups but, as Tom began to move off, Eve tentatively put her hand on his arm.

'Why, Tom?'

To her relief he didn't pretend to misunderstand her.

'Because—as I said—you're a qualified nurse, and small, and because…' He lifted his shoulders awkwardly. 'Yesterday, I said some totally unforgivable things to you, and apologising… You know I'm not good with words. If you want cutting and cruel, then I was taught by the best, but saying I'm sorry…'

'You don't have to say anything,' she said softly, and saw a muscle clench in his cheek.

'I do, but now's not the time to discuss it. I just wanted you to know…' He bit his lip. 'Asking for you, I hoped maybe you might see…'

'An olive branch?' she said. 'Seen, and accepted, Tom. Now, tell me how these thermal imaging cameras work.'

For a second he gazed at her silently, then he smiled.

'You're something else, Eve Dwyer.'

'Lippy, irritating, argumentative—yeah, I know,' she said lightly, unnerved by the intensity of his gaze, 'and you still haven't told me what a thermal imaging camera does.'

His smile widened.

'They detect and produce images of radiation, and since infrared radiation is emitted by all objects based on their temperatures, warm objects stand out well against cool backgrounds so humans and other warm-blooded animals become easily visible whether it's day or night.'

'Clever,' she said with admiration.

'Very.' He nodded, then his smile faded. 'Of course they can only pick up images of living things.'

'You think…' She swallowed. 'You think they might all be dead?'

'I think we have to be prepared for that given the silence.'

'The silence?' she repeated.

'Eve, if you were trapped, what would you be doing?'

'I'd be… Oh, I see,' she said with dawning comprehension. 'I'd be yelling my head off to attract attention, but nobody's yelling.'

'Exactly.'

She hoped he was wrong. She hoped it even more as the morning crept by with a painstaking slowness she found frustrating as Tom and his men scanned every square foot of rubble in Fisherman's Row with their cameras, and then checked and double-checked the results with a sound detector and fibreoptic probe.

'You thought a rescue operation would be a lot more exciting,' he observed with a slight smile, correctly reading her mind when he ordered his men to take a break. 'With people rushing from place to place.'

She coloured. 'I suppose so.'

'Sometimes it's like that,' he admitted. 'If a lot of people are trapped you can come upon them quite quickly, but when it's just three we have to take it slowly in case we miss something, plus there are a lot of potential hazards. Standing water can be electrically charged from underground or downed power lines, and we don't know how much untreated raw sewage there is in the water, not to mention the biohazards of dead animals, rotting food and liquid petroleum gases.'

She shivered as she stared up at the water line which showed how high the floodwater had reached in Fisherman's Row, and she knew it had been even higher in Bridge Street and Gull Close.

'I don't know how you can do this over and over again.'

'Somebody has to,' Tom observed.

'I know, but…'

She shivered again and, as though on cue, one of Tom's men appeared carrying a tray of steaming white polystyrene cups.

'What's this?' she asked, screwing up her nose after she'd taken a sip.

'Hot water, with three sugars,' the man replied, and she grimaced.

'I'd rather have a coffee,' she observed, and Tom grinned.

'Wouldn't we all, but both coffee and tea have caffeine in them, and that's a no-no because caffeine dehydrates you, and as we're all dehydrating rather a lot because we're sweating we don't want to add to it.'

'I'd still rather have a coffee,' she said with feeling as she sipped the hot water. 'Do you suppose…?' She came to a halt, seeing a dog appear at the top of Fisherman's Row. 'Tom, isn't that Foxy—Audrey's dog?'

He nodded as his eyes followed hers.

'Which would suggest Audrey is somewhere nearby. Dogs have a much more highly developed sense of smell than we do, and… Oh, hell.'

'What?' Eve said, in confusion, seeing Tom throw down his polystyrene cup, his face grim.

'He's pawing at the rubble by the Anchor Hotel. I think we may have found Audrey.'

They'd also found Reverend Kenner, too.

'My guess is the lady lost her footing when the river burst its banks,' Mitch declared. 'The reverend was holding her round the waist, so I'd say he was trying to keep her head above water, and then the outer wall of the hotel came down on them.'

Foxy was howling at the top of his lungs, desperately trying to get to his mistress, and Eve turned away quickly, not wanting anyone to see the tears that had filled her eyes at the sight of the two covered bodies lying on stretchers, but an arm came round her shoulders instantly.

'I shouldn't have asked you to do this,' Tom murmured. 'I'll get Mitch to take you back to the surgery.'

'No,' Eve insisted, wiping her sleeve across her eyes. 'Sophie is still missing so I'm not giving up. I just need…' Her voice became suspended, and she took a ragged breath. 'Why, Tom? Daniel Kenner… He was such a good man, such a kind man, and now Rachel has no father, her child will have no grandfather, and Audrey… Yes, she was a gossip, but to die like that… Why do some people live, and some people die, Tom?'

'An old Buddhist monk once told me that for some people it's simply their time,' Tom said, drawing her closer.

'It isn't for everyone—not always,' she said with difficulty, and she knew he understood what she meant because she felt his chin come to rest on the top of her head.

'Sufficient unto the day, Eve,' he said, his voice as uneven as hers. 'Sometimes that's all any of us can hold on to.'

'Tom, I...' She looked up at him, begging him to believe her, to understand. 'I didn't want to do it. Our baby. I truly didn't want to do it.'

'I know,' he said, his voice thick. Gently, he smoothed her hair back from her face with his fingers. 'Eve...' A loud blast from a whistle rent the air, and he turned towards it immediately. 'Someone's found a live one.'

He and Mitch were off and running before Eve could say anything, and by the time she'd caught up with them near the top of Bridge Street they were already deep in conversation with the man Tom had called Gregory.

'Is it Sophie?' she asked breathlessly as she stumbled to a halt beside them.

'Yes.'

Something about Tom's tone made her heart clutch.

'But I thought— One blast of the whistle—doesn't that mean she's alive?' she said.

'She is, but she's in big trouble,' Tom replied.

'I have glucagon in here,' Eve said, opening the medi-bag that Mitch had given her. 'If her blood-sugar levels are too low, and she's become hypoglycaemic—'

'She had the presence of mind to keep taking her glucagon, at least at the beginning,' Tom interrupted, 'but she was spending her day off school hiding out in one of the concrete sheds at the back of Bridge Street. That's why it's taken us so long to find her because Mitch and his men were concentrating on scanning the houses first.'

'And?' Eve demanded, wishing he would get to the point.

'When the shed flooded, part of it came down trapping Sophie by her leg.'

And not just trapping her by the leg, Eve realised when she followed the men down the narrow alley way to get to the back of the houses in Bridge Street. The piece of concrete had also come down at a right angle so all that was visible of the teenager was her head and upper body, and only somebody small would have any chance of being able to crawl close enough to her to assess her medical condition.

'It will have to be me, won't it?' Eve declared, cutting right across Mitch and Tom as they discussed how Tom might reach the girl. 'Look, you said one of the reasons you wanted me was because I'm a fully qualified nurse, and I'm small,' she continued, seeing Tom's eyebrows snap down, 'so it has to be me, doesn't it?'

'But if the rest of the shed comes down…' Tom said, indecision plain on his face.

'Tom, the longer we stand here debating this, the more likely it is that it *will* come down,' she said.

'She's right, Tom,' Mitch declared, and Eve saw Tom's eyebrows knit together still further.

'OK,' he said with clear reluctance, 'but if the shed begins to move I want your promise you'll get out of there.'

'I promise,' Eve said.

'Show me your hands.'

'What?'

'Eve, I know you've got your fingers crossed behind your back,' he declared, 'so let me see your hands when you promise.'

'OK—OK—I promise, no fingers crossed, and now can we get on with this?' she exclaimed, but she didn't feel anything like as confident when she began crawling under the concrete to get to the teenager.

Not only was the space a lot smaller than it looked, the water was filthy, and when she felt something brush against her leg and realised it was a dead rat, it took all of her self-control not to scuttle back out and run screaming from the building.

'Are you OK?' Tom called when she let out a gasp and Eve gritted her teeth until they hurt.

'Fine,' she said, but she felt even less fine after she'd examined the teenager.

Sophie was barely conscious and didn't even seem to be aware she was there and with a temperature of 91°F, and a GCS of 3-3-4, the girl was very ill indeed.

'I think she must be losing a lot of blood from her leg,' Eve said, and saw Tom shake his head.

'I think she's losing some, but not enough to cause those Glasgow coma scale results,' he replied. 'My guess is the main problem is she's been lying in freezing water for the past twenty-one hours.'

'A thermic lance,' Mitch declared. 'It's the only way, Tom.'

'What's a thermic lance?' Eve asked, glancing from Mitch to Tom, and it was Tom who answered.

'Basically, it's a long iron tube packed with a mixture of iron and aluminum rods. We feed oxygen through the tube, and when it's lit, it produces an intense flame that can cut through steel and concrete, but...'

'But?' Eve prompted.

'I don't know whether it will be able to cut through fast enough,' Tom said, 'and if it does whether the two halves will split away from her leg or impact down on her.'

'Tom, if we don't do something soon I think the question of what way the concrete might fall will be academic,' Eve replied. 'Her temperature's falling all the time.'

'OK, we use the thermic lance,' he said. 'Try to keep her awake, Eve. Sing to her—talk to her—but somehow keep her awake.'

It was easier said than done, Eve thought as Tom and Mitch began using the thermic lance to cut through the concrete that was pinning Sophie to the floor. Never had time seemed to pass so slowly as she crouched beneath the concrete, talking about everything and nothing while Sophie became increasingly unresponsive.

'Tom, her pulse ox is 80, her temperature's now 88, and she's not shivering any more,' Eve reported.

Because Sophie was developing hypothermia.

Neither she nor Tom said it, but they both knew it, and if Sophie's temperature continued to fall she'd start developing cardiac arrhythmias, then her heart would begin to fibrillate, and if her temperature slipped below 82°F there would be no way back for her.

'Fifteen minutes,' Tom replied in answer to Eve's unspoken question. 'We should be through the concrete in fifteen minutes.'

'Tom, I don't think she's going to hold on for fifteen minutes,' Eve said, and he let out a colourful oath.

'I know,' he exclaimed, 'but my only other alternative is to amputate her leg, and she's a kid, Eve, just a kid.'

But Sophie was going to die if she stayed in this water for much longer, Eve thought, and her feelings must have been all too apparent, because Tom thrust a dirt-grimed hand through his hair.

'Five minutes, Eve. Five minutes, and if we're no further forward, we amputate.'

She nodded and, as the seconds ticked by, she prayed as she had never prayed before. Prayed that the concrete would split in two soon. Prayed that Sophie would survive because there was no guarantee, no matter what they did, that she would. The girl was virtually comatose now, and her lips were beginning to turn blue which was a sure sign of cyanosis.

'It's moving, Tom,' Mitch shouted. 'The bloody thing's finally moving!'

Without a word Tom immediately crawled as far under the concrete as he could get, and Eve knew why. If the concrete fell on them he intended taking the full brunt of the fall, and her heart stopped for a second at the thought of him being crushed, of him dying in front of her eyes, and then—miraculously—

she saw a rush of bubbles in the water and Sophie sagged in her arms.

'She's free—I think she's free,' she declared, holding onto the girl for all she was worth, and Tom scrambled to his feet and splashed through the water towards her.

'Mitch, where's your chopper?' he demanded as he gripped Sophie under the armpits.

'The playing fields,' the pilot replied.

'Crank it up. This girl needs a hospital, and fast.'

Mitch couldn't have been faster. Within a short time he had Sophie and Tom airborne and in less than half an hour the girl was being admitted to St Piran's Hospital.

'Tom and his men—they're quite something, aren't they?' Lauren said when Eve told her about it later. 'It's not a job I'd like to do, but if I was ever in trouble I'd want the men from Deltaron coming over the horizon.'

And especially Tom, Eve thought as she helped the physiotherapist ensure that those who had sheltered in the school hall last night, and those who had taken refuge in The Smugglers', had all been allocated temporary accommodation in order to leave the hall free for Tom's men. He must have been exhausted when Mitch brought him back to Penhally but he'd stopped only long enough to tell them that the A and E consultant was hopeful Sophie would make a complete recovery and then he'd gone back out onto the streets with his men.

'I just wish I could find somewhere other than Harbour View for Miss Stanbury to stay in temporarily,' Lauren continued. 'There's no room left at The Smugglers', and I've put my foot down over a caravan, but she's such an independent woman, and staying in the nursing-home even for a short time… The last thing I want is her losing confidence in her ability to cope.'

'Who's losing confidence?'

Eve turned quickly at the familiar voice, and try as she may she couldn't prevent her heart lifting when she saw Tom smiling down at her.

'It's Miss Stanbury,' Lauren said, and after she'd explained the situation Tom shook his head.

'Not a nursing-home, not for Gertie. She can stay in my father's house in Trelissa Road. It's fully furnished, so she'll be quite snug and comfortable until her own home dries out.'

'Are you sure?' Lauren declared. 'I mean, lovely lady though Miss Stanbury is, I don't know what she would be like to share a house with and you'll be staying in your father's house yourself, won't you, now that the Anchor Hotel is uninhabitable?'

'Actually I won't,' he replied. 'I've made other arrangements.'

'Really?' Lauren exclaimed and, when Tom nodded, she beamed. 'Then you must come and tell her about your kind offer. She'll be so grateful.'

'Can't you tell her?' he said, already beginning to back awkwardly towards the school-hall door. 'I'm a bit tired—thought I might just head off, grab some sleep.'

He was out of the hall before Lauren could say anything else, and Eve laughed when she caught up with him.

'You fraud,' she declared. 'You just don't like people thanking you, do you?'

To her surprise, a faint wash of colour appeared on his cheeks.

'Not really, no.'

'And what are these other arrangements you've made?' she demanded, and saw Tom give a shamefaced grin.

'None, to be honest, but I can think of nothing I'd like less than staying in my father's old house, plus Gertie did me a good turn in the past and I figure it's time I repaid the debt. I can sleep in the hall with my men. It's no big deal, Eve,' he continued as she began to protest. 'I'll be perfectly fine.'

'I'm sure you will but not when there's an alternative,' she said firmly. 'My house has two bedrooms and you're more than welcome to use one of them. If…if you want to, that is,' she added, feeling her cheeks heat up when he stared at her in obvious surprise.

'I'd love to,' he said, 'but have you considered what people might say?'

'Tom, half of Penhally is covered in mud, silt and boulders. Half of the population are either sleeping with friends, or in a caravan, or at The Smugglers'. If anyone has the time or the energy to check up on where you're staying, then they need to get a life.'

He laughed.

'Well, if you're sure?'

'I'm sure,' she said. 'I can't offer you much to eat, but…' Her gaze took in his dirt-smeared face and hair, and bloodshot and weary eyes. 'I can offer you a bath.'

'You can heat water?' he said, his eyes lighting up, and she nodded.

'My dad installed a generator years back. He said he didn't much care if he couldn't watch TV when we had a power cut, but he was damned if he was going to sit in the dark, unable to have a bath.' She took a deep breath. 'I only have one condition to make.'

Tom grinned. 'Don't use all the hot water?'

She smiled. 'OK, two conditions. Don't use all the hot water, and…' Her smile faded. 'We don't talk about…about the baby. I know you want to,' she added quickly, seeing a flash of pain in his eyes, 'and I know we have to but, please, not tonight.'

He looked at her for a long moment, then smiled slightly crookedly.

'OK, not tonight,' he said.

'How do you feel now?' Eve asked when Tom joined her some time later in her small sitting room.

'A lot cleaner, that's for sure,' he said. 'I used some of your shampoo—I hope that was OK. Unfortunately you don't seem to have a razor so I couldn't get rid of this,' he added, rubbing his hand over the stubble on his chin, 'which means you'll have to put up with me looking scruffy.'

Or downright sexy, she thought, and stamped on the thought quickly as she put another log on the fire.

'Lauren and Chloe organised a clothes and general toiletries collection today for the people who can't get back into their homes,' she said. 'I should have thought to ask them to make up a bag for you, but I'm afraid I forgot you must have lost everything in the Anchor.'

'It doesn't matter,' he said dismissively. 'I've my wallet and my car keys. Everything else can be replaced.' He looked round awkwardly. 'Is there anything I can do—something to help?'

Aside from trying not to look quite so big, or so very immediate? she thought, but she didn't say that.

'Not really,' she said instead. 'I thought I would just heat up some soup, put it into a couple of mugs, and we could have it in here. It's warmer by the fire than in the kitchen.'

'Sounds good to me.' He nodded. 'Has Rachel Kenner been told about her father?'

'Nick went to see her this afternoon. As you can imagine…' Eve shook her head. 'It wasn't very pleasant, but Rachel's aunt and uncle have come over from Plymouth to stay with her. Audrey had no immediate family, but she had a sister who lives in Devon and we're trying to trace her.'

He sat down on the sofa and let his head fall back against it. 'God, but I'm tired.'

He looked tired. He also looked rumpled, and sloppy, and more attractive than any man had any right to be, and she put another log on the fire even though it didn't need it.

'When do you think they'll be able to restore the electricity to the village?' she asked.

'Perhaps tomorrow. Then we can send in the fire brigade to begin draining the houses, and my work will be done.'

*And I'll leave*.

He hadn't said the words, he didn't need to, and of course he would leave. He was only still here in Penhally because of the flood so it had been stupid of her heart to dip at his words but she couldn't deny it had dipped.

'Eve?'

He was gazing at her questioningly, and she forced herself to smile.

'I'll get the soup,' she said, but when she went into the kitchen she leant against the table and closed her eyes.

How had he managed to slip so easily back into her life? She'd always sworn she'd never let him get close to her again and yet, within the space of a few short days, it was almost as though he'd never been away, but he was going to leave again as he'd done before, and she was going to be alone again as she had been before.

Which was how it had to be, she told herself. Yes, she felt the old attraction—he had been right about that—but there was too much hurt and pain between them now and, even if he could eventually forgive her for what she had done, he had his life, and she had hers, and their time was past.

Except it wasn't that easy, she realised, when she went back into the sitting room with their soup and she found him fast asleep on the sofa.

Twenty years. It had been twenty years since they'd last met, and yet she only had to see him like this, his face so tired in the firelight, his hair still damp from his bath, his eyelashes dark against his skin, and she wanted him all over again. Wanted to go to him, to wrap her arms around him, to have him hold her as he used to.

*You can't go back, Eve*, her heart whispered, and yet before she could stop herself she had carefully put the soup down on the mantelpiece, and just as carefully stretched out her hand, meaning only to smooth his hair back from his forehead, but he was a light sleeper and his eyes flew open with a start.

'I'm sorry,' she said awkwardly, backing up a step. 'I didn't mean to wake you.'

'It's just as well you did,' he said ruefully. 'I never could fall asleep in a chair without waking up with an infernal crick in my neck.'

'Snap.' She laughed as she handed him a mug of soup, but to her surprise he didn't join in her laughter.

Instead, he stared down at his soup, then up at her.

'I'm thinking of resigning from Deltaron, Eve. Maybe going into general practice.'

Her mouth fell open, then she shook her head.

'Tom, you'd be bored witless in under a week,' she protested. 'You're used to immediacy, constant change. I know you said you were worried you were ceasing to care but, believe me, GP work is not for you.'

'Perhaps not,' he murmured, his face all dark planes and shadows in the firelight. 'But... I used to get such a buzz from the danger, Eve, from pitting myself against the elements—fire, flood, earthquake—and yet now... All the time I'm thinking, What if I get it wrong, make a mistake, miscalculate?'

'You haven't yet.'

His face darkened still further.

'I have.'

His voice was so low she barely heard him, and for a second she hesitated then she sat down on the sofa beside him.

'What happened, Tom?'

She didn't think he was going to answer, then he put his soup down on the floor beside him and gripped his knees.

'We were sent to India last year to help out after a very bad earthquake. The village we were assigned to had been pretty well flattened, but one house was still standing, and we could hear people calling for help from inside it. I knew…' Tom took in an uneven breath. 'I knew the house was unstable, that it could go at any minute, but I could hear kids crying so I took the gamble it would hold.'

She reached out and laced one of her hands with his, and held it tightly.

'Go on,' she said.

'Charlie Dobbs, the other medic on the team, and I went in,' he continued with an effort. 'We'd just reached the kids—I had actually caught hold of one of their hands—and the house collapsed. I was pulled out alive, but Charlie, the people, the kids, they were all killed.'

'It wasn't your fault, Tom,' she said softly. 'You were trying to give them a chance, and Charlie… He would have known the risks, just as you did.'

'That's what the head of Deltaron said,' he declared, his eyes desolate, 'but I keep thinking if I'd done it differently, maybe tried to shore up the house, maybe waited…'

'You did what you thought was right at the time, Tom,' she said, hating to see the torment in his eyes. 'That's all anybody can do.'

'I went to Charlie's funeral,' he continued as though she hadn't spoken. 'Deltaron flew his body back to the States, so I went to his funeral and there was nobody there but me and the minister. He had no brothers or sisters, and his parents were both dead, so it was just me and the minister standing at the graveside, and I thought…' He swallowed. 'I thought, One day that's going to be me.'

'No, it won't,' she insisted, but he shook his head.

'It will, Eve. I've given my whole life to the company, just as Charlie did, so one day I'll be buried with no one there to mourn me, nobody who cares enough about me to come and say goodbye.'

'I'll come, Tom,' she said, her lip trembling. 'You wouldn't be alone. I'd come.'

'But you wouldn't know, Eve,' he said, his eyes meeting hers, dark and empty. 'You'd be here in Penhally, and I could be anywhere in the world.'

'Tom—'

'Eve, there's something I have to tell you,' he interrupted. 'Something I want you to know. Do you remember when I said I had two reasons for coming back to Penhally? Well, the other reason…' He came to a halt with a muttered oath as his mobile phone began to ring, and impatiently he pulled it from his pocket, checked the caller ID, then punched the answer button. 'Mitch, this had better be important,' he said.

It clearly was, Eve thought as she watched the frown lines on Tom's forehead deepen at whatever the pilot was saying, and when the call was over Tom immediately got to his feet.

'Bad news?' she said uncertainly.

'They've found a fractured gas main in Gull Close,' he replied. 'I have to go.'

'But you're exhausted,' she protested, 'and you're not an engineer. Can't somebody else deal with it?'

'I'm the boss, Eve, so I have to be there. Don't wait up for me. I don't know how long I'm going to be.'

'Right,' she said, then added quickly before she could stop herself, 'Be careful.'

'I fully intend to,' he said with a small smile, 'because we have a conversation to finish, and I intend finishing it.'

And, to her surprise, he bent down and kissed her lightly on the forehead, then strode out of her sitting room, leaving her gazing open-mouthed after him.

# CHAPTER SEVEN

THE WAITING room was crammed to overflowing with press people, and each and every one of them seemed to be armed with a camera, a notebook and an apparently unending supply of stupid questions.

'I wonder how long it's going to be before Nick hits someone,' Dragan murmured as he and Eve stood outside in the surgery corridor watching Tom, Nick, and Chief Constable D'Ancey field questions.

'I should imagine just until one of those reporters asks him—yet again—whether he's sure there's only been two fatalities,' Eve said dryly.

'Or maybe until someone asks him for yet another photograph of him and Tom shaking hands,' Dragan declared, and Eve let out a small choke of laughter.

'Yup, I reckon that would probably do it.'

'Ghouls,' Dragan said with distaste. 'The whole pack of them are nothing but ghouls. The paparazzi came out in droves when they found out about Melinda and me, but this…' He shook his head. 'I don't know how Tom keeps his temper when you consider how many of these press conferences he must have taken part in.'

'I suppose because he has to,' Eve murmured, glancing back into the waiting room and seeing Tom wearily rotate his shoulders, his face a carefully arranged expressionless mask. 'I think Tom has learned to do a lot of things because he has to.'

Including having to accept he wasn't God, she thought sadly, with all the attendant heartbreak that knowledge could bring.

'Looks like Nick's just reached breaking point,' Dragan said when the senior partner suddenly stood up, his face dark and stormy. 'Yup, he's reached it, and I think he's actually passed it.'

The senior partner had. With an angry nod at Chief Constable D'Ancey, Nick strode out of the waiting room without a backward glance and, when he went into his consulting room, he slammed the door so hard it shuddered.

'It doesn't look as though Nick has enjoyed his encounter with the members of the press, does it?' Kate said, her eyes dancing as she joined them.

'Perhaps it will teach him to have a little more sympathy for Tom in future,' Eve replied before she could stop herself, and the midwife laughed.

'We can but hope,' she said. 'Do you think we might be able to get on with afternoon surgery soon?' she continued as the press began to file out of the waiting room 'I know the press is entitled to a story, but we've told them all we know, and what we need now is to try to get back to some sort of normality, and that means seeing patients.'

'I couldn't agree more,' Dragan replied, 'and in that spirit I'll be in my consulting room if anyone wants me.'

'And I'll be in my examination room,' Kate declared as Dragan disappeared, 'hoping at least some of my mums-to-be manage to make it down for their prenatal check-ups.'

'Is the embargo on evening home visits still in place?' Eve asked, and Kate sighed.

'Nick is adamant that unless it's an emergency none of us are to be out after dark, and he's even more against it since Lauren took a tumble yesterday. I know it makes sense,' Kate continued. 'Some of the pavements and roads in Penhally are lethal, but I have quite a few my mums-to-be who can't come in during the day because they're at work.'

'Do you think…?' Eve began, then stopped. Chloe and Oliver were walking down the corridor towards them and it was obvious from the woman's stricken countenance that something was badly wrong. 'Chloe, are you all right?'

'She insisted I take her down to Fisherman's Row this morning,' Oliver replied, 'and she's a bit upset by what she saw.'

'Chloe, your home can be repaired,' Eve said quickly. 'Tom said once all the mud and silt have been pumped out—'

'It's not the house,' Chloe interrupted. 'That's just bricks and mortar, but Cyclops and Pirate… Eve, there's no sign of them, anywhere.'

'Cats have nine lives, babe, you know that,' her fiancé said, putting his arm around her and giving her a hug. 'They're probably just hiding out some place, too scared to come home.'

'Truly?' Chloe said, and, when Oliver nodded, she gave a wobbly smile. 'You think I'm being stupid, don't you?'

'Babe, you could never be stupid,' he said gently. 'They'll be fine. I know they will.'

But he wasn't, Eve knew, as Chloe and Kate hurried away to start their afternoon clinic, and she knew why. The water level in Oliver and Chloe's home must have reached nine feet at the flood's height, and neither Cyclops nor Pirate were robust cats.

'What's the matter with Chloe?' Tom asked as he joined them. 'She looks as though she's lost a pound and found a penny.'

'It's her cats,' Eve replied and, after she'd explained, Tom frowned.

'So, Cyclops is a ginger cat and only has one eye, and Pirate is white with a black patch over one eye. OK, I'll ask my men to keep a special watch out for them.'

'Yeah, right,' Oliver muttered, but Tom heard him.

'Oliver, I know your opinion of me is about as low as it can be,' he said without heat, 'but when I make a promise I keep it.'

'Right,' Oliver said, his cheeks darkening slightly. 'Sorry,' he added, but as Tom turned to go, the junior doctor held out his hand to stay him. 'Look, I truly am sorry, Tom, and not just for the cats. On the night of the flood, I said some pretty appalling things to you—'

'Forget it,' Tom interrupted.

'Yes, but—'

'Forget it,' Tom repeated. 'We were all a bit fraught that night, and if someone I loved had been missing I would have behaved exactly as you did.'

'Yes, well…' Oliver thrust his fingers through his hair awkwardly. 'It's good of you to say so, and considerably more than I deserve. If your men do find the cats, and they're dead, could you tell me first? I don't want Chloe to see them looking… messed up. She…' His shoulders lifted helplessly. 'They mean so much to her, you see.'

'Not a problem,' Tom replied but, after Oliver had gone, Eve folded her arms across her chest and shook her head at him.

'He owes you a much bigger apology than that,' she said, and saw one corner of Tom's mouth lift.

'Eve, people say things in the heat of the moment, and I have broad enough shoulders and a thick enough skin to cope with it. Oliver was worried sick about Chloe that night, and if I'd been in his shoes I would probably have said a hell of a lot more.'

'Even so,' she protested, 'I still feel—'

'Plus, I hardly think I'm in a position to criticise somebody else's thoughtless words, do you?' he interrupted.

His eyes were fixed on her, and she felt a faint wash of colour creep across her cheeks.

'Tom…'

'I know.' He nodded. 'Not here, not now, but we're going to have to talk about it some time, Eve.'

She knew they would, but she didn't want to talk about it because talking changed nothing, altered nothing. Talking simply meant she had to relive it again, and she'd relived it so often in her mind—regretted it so often.

'Do you know what's going to happen to Audrey's dog, Foxy?' she said, deliberately changing the subject, and knew from the way Tom shook his head that he wasn't deceived for a second.

'The RSPCA is looking after him at the moment,' he replied, 'but to be honest they're a bit worried about him. He's not eaten anything since they picked him up, and there's no doubt he's going to be difficult to rehome because people generally want puppies, not older dogs. I'd take him myself, but the RSPCA say he's wary of men, plus a dog really shouldn't have a globe-trotting owner. Maybe if I had a wife, a family…'

His words hung in the air between them, and Eve plucked at a loose thread on her sleeve.

'I hope you find someone one day, Tom,' she murmured. 'You deserve to be happy.'

'But you don't think you do.'

The unexpectedness of his comment completely threw her.

'Of—of course I deserve to be happy,' she stammered, 'and I *am* happy. I have my work, and Tassie, and…' Desperately she tried to think of something else that made her happy but to her dismay her mind seemed suddenly blank. 'I'm *happy*, Tom.'

'Eve, you need more in your life than your work, and looking after someone else's child once a week,' he said gently, 'but until you let go of the past, move on, you're not going to believe that. You're going to continue to keep people at arm's length because you don't think you're entitled to happiness.'

'I— You—you're talking nonsense,' she said vehemently. 'You're making it sound as though—'

She didn't get an opportunity to finish what she'd been about to say. Dragan had appeared, looking white-faced and tense.

'I've just had a phone call from Melinda,' he said unevenly. 'Her waters have broken. She's having the baby, Eve, and it's two weeks early.'

'Which is no time at all,' she said soothingly. 'In fact, she probably got her dates wrong—it's not uncommon.'

'Right,' he said, though Eve doubted whether he'd actually heard her. 'I need to go to her, but I have surgery this afternoon— My patients—'

'I'll take your place,' Tom interrupted. 'I'm a fully qualified doctor, remember, and I'm sure Nick wouldn't object.'

To Eve's amazement the senior partner didn't. He simply gave Tom a long, appraising stare, then nodded.

'Just so long as you realise what you're letting yourself in for,' he said. 'General practice is not for everyone.'

'Then it's OK if I go?' Dragan said, clearly anxious to leave, and Nick gave him a gentle push with his finger.

'Of course you can go, you idiot. Give Melinda my best, and try not to faint. It reflects badly on the practice.'

Quickly, Dragan strode to the door, then came back and gripped Tom's hands.

'*Bog te blagoslovio!*' the Croatian doctor exclaimed. '*Hvala*, Tom. I just want to say—*hvala*.'

'Do you have any idea what he said?' Tom asked, bemused, when Dragan had rushed away.

'I imagine he was thanking you,' Eve declared, 'but I'm afraid I can't give you an exact translation as I don't speak Croatian.'

Tom grinned. 'In which case he could have been telling me in no uncertain terms to…um…remove myself.'

'Maybe somebody should,' she muttered, and walked off to her examination room, but Tom came after her.

'Eve, what I said earlier—about you needing to move on— I'm sorry if you feel I spoke out of turn.'

*If*, she thought angrily. How dared he imply—suggest—she was some lonely, unhappy woman, stuck in the past, who had spent the last twenty years punishing herself for what she'd done? She may not be able to forgive herself, but she'd created a full life, a satisfying life, and she was on her own through choice. Not everyone met someone they wanted to spend the rest of their life with. A lot of luck was involved, like being in the right place at the right time.

Like you and Tom, her heart whispered, and she crushed down the thought immediately.

'As you appear to make a habit of speaking out of turn, I don't suppose I should be surprised,' she said tightly.

'Eve, I was only speaking as I see it,' he protested, and she shook her head.

'Isn't that what people with big mouths, and even bigger egos, usually say to justify sticking their noses into other people's business?'

He opened his mouth, then closed it again.

'Fair point,' he declared. 'In future I will button my lip whenever I feel the urge to make any kind of observation.'

'You couldn't button your lip if your life depended on it!' she exclaimed, and saw his eyes twinkle.

'No, but I'm prepared to swear anything to get back into your good graces.'

He was gazing at her with a quite ludicrously hangdog expression, and anger warred with amusement inside her for a moment and amusement won.

'You're impossible, Tom Cornish. You know that, don't you?' she said.

'Yup.' He grinned. 'But I got you to laugh.'

'I don't think you're going to be laughing by the end of this afternoon,' she observed. 'In fact… Look, are you sure you know what you're doing—volunteering to take Dragan's clinic?'

He groaned. 'Not you, too. It's bad enough having Nick doubt my professional capabilities—'

'It's not your professional capabilities I'm worried about,' she interrupted, 'and I don't think it's what Nick is concerned about either. It's been a long time since you've met "ordinary" members of the public, Tom, and I think you're in for quite an eye-opener.'

Tom rolled his eyes with exasperation, but it didn't take him long to discover both she and Nick were right. He could tolerate the stream of people he saw that afternoon who had met with unfortunate accidents due to the uneven roads and pavements, but what he found impossible to cope with were the people who appeared to have blithely ignored every health leaflet Nick had sent out, and now felt distinctly aggrieved because they weren't feeling well.

'Is it my imagination or is the entire world populated by complete idiots?' he demanded, by the end of the afternoon. 'There's been a flood, the water supply has been contaminated, Nick has issued leaflets advising people to drink bottled water, and yet what do some people do?'

'You tell me,' Eve said, her lips twitching as her gaze took in his distinctly frazzled expression.

'They drink water out of the tap,' Tom retorted. 'They come in here, saying, "I thought it looked all right, Doctor, and now I've got a fever, and a really bad headache." Well, of course they have. The prats have contracted Weil's disease.'

'And did you tell them they were prats?' Eve asked, controlling the laughter she could feel bubbling up inside her with difficulty.

'No, but it was a close-run thing,' he admitted. 'And do you know how many people I saw this afternoon who decided it would be a whiz bang idea to light a camp stove to speed up the drying out of their houses?' he continued. '*Three*, Eve. That's three idiots who now have carbon-monoxide poisoning because they were too lazy, or too dim, to read the warning leaflets which specifically said the fumes from charcoal were deadly.'

'Oh, dear,' she said unevenly, and he gave her a hard stare.
'It is *not* funny, Eve.'

'The illnesses certainly aren't, but your face sure is,' she said
with a peal of laughter. 'I'm sorry, Tom. It's not fair of me to
mock,' she continued as his eyebrows snapped together, 'but
Nick and I did try to warn you that general practice wasn't for
you.'

He thrust his fingers through his hair, making it stand out all
over the place, then smiled reluctantly.

'OK—all right—so you were both right, and I was wrong.
Maybe becoming a GP would be a bad career move for me.'

'If you were on the verge of strangling the patients you saw
after just one afternoon, then it sure would be,' she replied.
'Deltaron is where you belong, Tom. I think you need a break—
a long holiday—but I think Deltaron is where you're meant to
be.'

'But only if I get myself a life outside my work, just as you
should.'

The smile on her face disappeared.

'I thought we agreed this subject was a no-go area?'

'Can't blame a bloke from trying.' He grinned, and she shook
her head at him.

'You're completely incorrigible.'

'I think that was one of the nicer things Gertie Stanbury used
to say about me when I was at school,' he replied. 'In fact—'

'The very person I wanted to see,' Lauren interrupted as she
came out of her physiotherapy room and saw them. 'Tom, I have
Miss Stanbury with me, and she'd very much like to thank you
personally for the loan of your house.'

That he didn't want to be thanked was plain. In fact, he had
the look of a man who would have preferred to have his toenails
pulled out, but Eve wasn't going to let him get away with it, at
least not this time.

'Tom, if she wants to thank you, you have to let her,' she

declared, and she saw reluctance and unwillingness war with each other on his face for a second, then he sighed.

'OK—all right,' he said.

'And I dare you to call her Gertie to her face,' Eve added in an undertone as she followed him down the corridor.

'Are you kidding?' he protested. 'I want to live to be fifty.'

Eve didn't think the elderly lady would have cared what Tom called her. She was far too overwhelmed by his generosity.

'It's almost like being at home,' she said, her small face wreathed in smiles, 'and I can't thank you enough for allowing me to stay there. I just hope I'm not inconveniencing you.'

'Not in the slightest,' Tom insisted. 'Stay for as long as you like, and most definitely until your own home is habitable again.'

'Amanda Lovelace drove me round to Gull Close this morning,' Gertrude continued. 'Seeing it... I can't believe Tassie and I got out of there alive.'

'It's not going to always look like that, Miss Stanbury,' Tom said softly, seeing the stricken look that had suddenly appeared in her eyes. 'Once the fire brigade has pumped out the water, and it's been dried out, you'll soon have it looking as it did before.'

'I just wish I'd thought to take my papers and photographs with me when I went up into the attic,' she said 'When I looked in the window, they were all there—floating about in the water.'

'Miss Stanbury—'

'I know—I know,' she interrupted as Tom looked at her with concern. 'The most important thing is Tassie and I are here to tell the tale. As for my photographs, papers...' Her lip trembled slightly, and she firmed it. 'Not important.'

Tom hunkered down on his heels in front of her, his green eyes soft with understanding.

'You haven't lost them,' he said. 'If this was the summer we could air-dry them for you in a trice but at the moment what we need is a freezer. If we can find someone with a big freezer, all we need to do is to pop your photographs and papers in, freeze them, and they can be air-dried when the weather is better.'

'And that will work?' Gertrude declared, and Eve could see hope stirring in the elderly lady's eyes.

'Yup,' Tom said, and Gertrude shook her head in amazement.

'The wonders of modern technology.'

'Nah.' Tom grinned. 'Knowledge gained from a misspent youth.'

Gertrude chuckled wryly.

'You haven't changed a bit, Tom Cornish,' she declared. 'You're just the same lippy, opinionated, and—' she stretched out and caught hold of one of his hands, and gripped it firmly in her own frail one '—downright kind and decent human being you always were.'

'And there was me thinking I had you fooled,' Tom said, his cheeks darkening, and Gertrude shook her head.

'Not for a minute, lad. Not for one single minute.'

'That was kind of you,' Eve said when she and Tom left the surgery some time later.

'I wasn't lying to Gertie,' Tom replied, taking hold of her elbow to steer her round the rubble in Harbour Road. 'She might not be able to save all of her photographs and private papers, but she should be able to salvage most.'

'I didn't mean that,' Eve said. 'I meant the way you talked to her. You've a good heart, Tom.'

'Anyone else would have done the same,' he said dismissively, but she could see the embarrassment back on his face again, and stared at him curiously.

'Why does gratitude make you so uncomfortable?' she said, and to her surprise he didn't meet her gaze.

'I guess…' Tom took an awkward breath. 'Maybe it's because my father always battered it into me when I was a kid that nobody does anything for nothing. "There's no such thing as a free lunch, Tom." That was one of his favourite sayings, so I suppose I find it hard to believe people are on the level.'

'Gertrude is, and she knows you are,' she said softly.

'I'd rather you did,' he said, turning to face her, and it was her turn to look away.

'Your promise didn't last very long,' she said.

'Yeah, well, never trust a Cornish.'

She could hear the laughter in his voice, and shook her head.

'Ain't that the truth,' she replied. 'Tony at The Smugglers' has huge freezers. I bet he'd offer to help Gertrude in an instant.'

'I understand he's doing very well in hospital,' Tom said, and Eve couldn't help but laugh.

'You mean, you've heard he's giving the staff merry hell, demanding to be discharged.'

'I heard that, too.' Tom grinned. 'I'm afraid he's going to have to take things a lot easier from now on whether he wants to or not.'

'I think this flood is going to change quite a few people's lives.' Eve sighed.

'I'm hoping so.'

His words were innocuous enough, but she wasn't deceived for a second.

'I thought we agreed—'

His green eyes met hers.

'You can run, Eve, but you can't hide.'

He was right, she thought, and his words became even more prophetic after they'd reached her cottage and she made them both a simple meal of pasta Bolognese. Every time she looked up his gaze was on her, thoughtful, pensive. Every time she tried to start a conversation, he answered her in monosyllables and she knew why. He was waiting. Waiting for her to talk about the baby, and though she knew they had to talk about it, she didn't want to see his eyes darken again with pain or to relive the decision she'd made all those years ago.

'Would you like anything else to eat?' she said hopefully after she'd gathered up their empty plates. 'I have cheese and biscuits, and I managed to get some fruit from the corner shop. Goodness knows how it survived the flood, but it did.'

'No, thank you,' he replied.

'A coffee, then?' she suggested, knowing her voice was beginning to sound slightly panic-stricken but quite unable to control it. 'It's only instant but—'

'I don't want a coffee, thank you,' he interrupted. 'What I want is to talk to you.'

'Tom, I'm really tired,' she said quickly. 'In fact, I thought I might actually have an early night.'

He got to his feet, took the plates from her hands and put them back on the table.

'Eve, I could get a call at any time from Deltaron,' he declared, 'and I don't want to leave Penhally without us having spoken about…about our child.'

He was right about the call, and she knew from his set expression he wasn't going to take no for an answer, but when she walked over to the sofa she sat down wearily.

'Tom, what is there left for us to say?' she murmured. 'I was pregnant, I decided I couldn't have the baby, I had an abortion. I know you must hate me for what I did—'

'I don't hate you,' he interrupted, sitting down beside her. 'Maybe I thought I did, when you first told me—when I thought of the son or daughter I could have had—but those thoughts were the thoughts of the man I am now. The man I was all those years ago would have felt only relief that you didn't have the baby.'

'Relief?' she echoed, and he took a deep breath.

She had opened her heart to him, told him everything, and she deserved the same truth from him no matter how badly it reflected upon him.

'Eve, I'm ashamed to admit it, but if I'm honest—and I want

to be completely honest with you—I wouldn't have wanted a baby, not then. I had this wonderful career, you see,' he continued, his mouth twisting into an ironic and bitter smile. 'I was Dr Tom Cornish, all set to conquer the world, and a baby... I would have seen a baby as an encumbrance, that I was being trapped into a responsibility I didn't want to have, just as my father was.'

'And now you wish I hadn't done it,' she murmured, pleating and unpleating her fingers, 'but I can't undo it, Tom, no matter how much I might want to. I was weak all those years ago, took the easy way out, just as you said I did.'

'Weak?' he exclaimed. 'Eve, you took the hardest decision anyone can ever make, and you took it alone. When I think of you going to the clinic by yourself...' He shook his head. 'No one should have to go through that alone, and yet you did. You were the one who possessed the strength all those years ago, not me.'

'It wasn't strength, Tom, it was cowardice,' she said, her voice raw, harsh. 'I was so desperate. Desperate and scared that I wouldn't be able to cope, and I wish—I so wish—I could go back, and do things differently, but all the wishing in the world isn't going to make that happen.'

Awkwardly, he half reached for her, but he didn't know whether she would reject his touch—not want it—so he clasped her hand in his instead.

'If anyone's to blame for what happened, it's me,' he insisted. 'You should have felt you could come to me, and the fact you didn't... I let you down, Eve. Me.'

'I don't even know whether we had a son or a daughter, Tom,' she said, her lips trembling. 'I felt—I don't know why—it was a little girl, but one of the nurses... She said it wasn't a baby, not a real baby, just a collection of cells. But it was a baby, Tom. Our baby—and I killed it.'

He felt his heart twist with pain, but what deepened the pain, intensified it, were the tears he could see shimmering in her eyes, tears he knew were going to fall at any moment, and holding her hand was not enough—not nearly enough—and he put his arm around her, drawing her close.

'Don't, Eve, *don't*,' he begged, hating to see her suffering, but she misunderstood him.

'It's the truth, Tom,' she said. 'I did it. It was my decision, not yours. Mine, and I want so much to say I'm sorry to our daughter, but I can't. There's not even a grave I can stand beside so I won't ever be able to tell our baby that I'm sorry, and some-times…'

The tears in her eyes overflowed, and Tom put his other arm round her, and held her tightly, his own throat constricted.

'Eve, listen to me,' he said into her hair. 'If we had made love ten years ago, and you'd discovered you were pregnant, would you have had an abortion?'

'Of course I wouldn't,' she said into his chest.

'Why not?' he said, knowing full well what her answer would be, but knowing, too, that he had to make her say it, see it.

'Because I had a good job ten years ago,' she exclaimed, 'and a flat of my own in Newquay!'

'None of which you had when you were twenty-two. Eve…' He clasped her face between his hands and forced her to look at him. 'You did what you thought was right twenty years ago, and now you have to forgive yourself, to move on, and believe you're entitled to a future, to happiness.'

'I don't know if I can,' she said brokenly.

He smoothed her hair back from her damp cheeks.

'You asked me—oh, it seems a lifetime ago now—why I came back to Penhally. I said I could give you one reason, but not the other—not then. Well, I can give you that other reason now. I came back because I've never stopped loving you.'

She stared at him in open-mouthed amazement for a full minute, then drew back from him.

'You're asking me to believe you've been in love with me for the past twenty years?' she exclaimed.

'Is that so very surprising?' he said.

It clearly was to her, he thought, seeing her shake her head, and her words confirmed it.

'Tom, if you'd truly felt like that you would have kept in touch,' she protested, 'but you never phoned, or wrote, or made any attempt to see me.'

'Because I was the one who walked away,' he said, willing her to believe him. 'I was the one who'd said I didn't want to be tied down, didn't want a wife or a family. You would have been quite within your rights to say, *On your bike, Tom Cornish*, and, as the years passed, I told myself you must be married, so I thought—I felt—I couldn't come back.'

'And you've been pining for me for the last twenty years?' she said, not bothering to hide her cynicism. 'I don't think so, Tom.'

'No, I haven't been pining for you for the last twenty years,' he admitted, 'but, because I made the biggest mistake of my life, I have spent those years trying to convince myself that the image I had of you couldn't be a real one, that no one could be so special, or different.'

'I'm not different, or special, Tom,' she said.

'You are, and because you are I kept on dating, and dating, and...' He broke off awkwardly, with a crooked smile and a gesture of dismissal. 'When none of my relationships worked out, I finally had to admit what I'd known all along. That I was looking for someone like you, and there wasn't anyone like you, there never could be.'

'So you came back to Penhally hoping to find me unhappily married, or divorced, so you could become involved with me again?' she said, outrage plain in her voice, and he swore under his breath.

Hell, was he never going to be able to find the right words to say to her? Was he doomed always to screw things up, and he was screwing things up, big time, because he see her barriers going up, and he couldn't lose her a second time, simply couldn't.

'It wasn't like that,' he said vehemently. 'I thought…' He grasped her hands before she could draw back, and held onto them. 'Part of me hoped to find you happily married because I thought—if you were—I might finally be able to move on, to bury the dream I had of somehow undoing the mistake I'd made, and the other part…I thought if you were still single that maybe…you and I…maybe we could try again.'

Her eyes met his, and he could read nothing of what she was thinking in them, and then she cleared her throat.

'Tom, have you thought that what you've been wanting back for all these years isn't me, but your youth and your dreams, and I can't give you that. No one can.'

'You said that to me before,' he said, willing her to see the truth in his eyes, 'but it isn't that, I know it isn't. Since we parted there's never been anybody in my life like you. There have been other women—I won't deny that—but it was always you. Nobody ever came anywhere close to you.'

Gently, she slipped her hands free from his.

'Even if I believed that, Tom,' she murmured. 'Even if what you say is true, we can't go back. You know we can't.'

'Why not?' he said.

It was a good question and one Eve wasn't entirely sure she could answer. She knew nobody had ever touched her heart the way he had, but she also knew no one had ever hurt her quite so much either, and to go down that road again, risk everything again…

'Tom, we're not the same people any more, and our worlds—they're too different, too far apart.'

'Then I'll give up working for Deltaron, and come back to Penhally,' he said. 'I'm getting too old to be traipsing around the world anyway, and after what happened last year in India—'

'And what would you do in Penhally?' she interrupted. 'This afternoon must have proved to you beyond a shadow of a doubt you'll never make a country GP, and Penhally… There are too many bad memories for you here. You'd never feel you belonged.'

'Then you could come to London with me,' he declared. 'Or there's my flat in Lausanne. You'd love Switzerland, Eve. It's a beautiful country, and if you wanted to continue nursing you'd easily find work there.'

He looked so desperate, so anxious, and she didn't want to hurt him, but she knew she must.

'Tom, my home is here,' she said. 'And to uproot myself from everything I know, from everyone I know on the strength of…'

'A whim?' he finished for her. 'It's not a whim, Eve, it's a question of trust. A question of whether you believe me when I say I love you and I always will.'

He made it sound so easy, so simple, but he'd made it sound easy and simple all those years ago, too.

'Let's have fun,' he'd said, and she'd thought they'd get married, raise a family in Penhally, and within a few short months her dreams and hopes had all been left lying shattered in the dust.

'I can't, Tom. And you're assuming too much,' she continued as he tried to interrupt. 'Assuming I still feel the same way about you.'

He reached out and gently cupped her cheek with his hand. 'Don't you?'

His eyes were deep and green and dark, and she shivered at the intensity she could see in them and, when he traced her neck with the fingers of his other hand, she shivered even more.

'It's still there, isn't it?' he continued, his voice suddenly deep, husky. 'What you used to feel for me, it's still there?'

'No,' she said, trying to sound firm but unfortunately her voice wobbled.

'Then, if I kiss you, you'll feel nothing?'

He didn't even need to kiss her, she thought. She could already feel herself melting, responding to him, wanting to touch him, to hold him, but she also knew nothing had been resolved between them, and it never could.

'Tom…I don't…I…'

'I'll take that as a yes,' he said, and bent his head towards her, and before she could say anything his lips met hers and she was lost.

Lost on a tide of need and longing. Lost in a sea of old memories, and sensations, and she slid her arms up his back to bring him closer, heard him groan against her mouth as he deepened the kiss, and he threaded his fingers through her hair so she couldn't escape, and she didn't want to escape.

'I have dreamt about doing this for so long,' he said, his breathing ragged. 'Wanted it, longed for it, and now you're here, in my arms, and it's right, so right.'

It felt right to her, too, as he smothered her face and neck with kisses, and when he slid his hands up under her sweater, and she felt the heat of his fingers through the lace of her bra, she arched against him, feeling her nipples harden instantly. It would be so easy to let go, she thought with a sigh as he drew her closer to him, and she felt his heart beating rapidly against hers, felt a heat begin to spread out deep and low in her stomach. It would be so easy simply to enjoy the moment, and it had been so long since she'd been in a man's arms, so long since she'd made love, but though her body and her heart spoke loudly, her head spoke louder still.

Nothing has changed, her mind warned, nothing *can* change. In a few days' time—probably less—he'll be gone, and then what? Then you'll be left with even more regret, even more memories to hurt you. With a sob, she pulled herself free from his arms and stood up.

'I can't,' she cried. 'I'm sorry, but I can't do this.'

'Eve—'

'I'm scared, Tom.'

'Of me?' he said in horror, and she shook her head as she wrapped her arms around herself.

'Of what will happen to me if I let you get close again. I can't go down that road and have you leave me again. I can't.'

'Why would you think I'd leave you?' he demanded.

'Because you always do,' she said, her voice trembling. 'You make me feel special, and different, and then you leave.'

'Eve, I *love* you,' he protested, reaching for her only to see her back away. 'I want us to be together for always. Can't you believe that?'

'I want to—I truly want to,' she said, 'but I can't risk it—I *can't*, Tom.'

'Eve, listen to me—'

'No,' she interrupted. 'No,' she repeated. 'You'll just talk me round like you always could. Go back to your world, Tom, and I'll stay in my own little one. I know it's not an exciting place like yours, and maybe…maybe it's not always completely fulfilling, but it's safe. It's never going to let me down, or walk away from me, and I have to have that kind of certainty, don't you see?'

'I can give you certainty,' he protested. 'Eve—'

'No, Tom,' she said, and before he could stop her she'd fled, and he swore long, and low, and fluently.

# CHAPTER EIGHT

'DOES anybody else have anything to add, or can I call this practice meeting to a close?' Nick said, leaning back in his chair.

'Has anyone heard anything from the hospital about Melinda?' Eve asked.

Nick shook his head.

'Dragan phoned Chloe a couple of hours ago, said he was hoping it wouldn't be too much longer, but we haven't heard anything since.'

'That must be—what?—nineteen hours now?' Oliver said.

'It's not unusual for first babies to take a while to arrive,' Chloe said calmly. 'I'm sure there's no need to worry.'

'I wouldn't tell Dragan that.' Her fiancé grinned. 'I bet the poor bloke's got no fingernails left.'

'I'm surprised Tom had any hair left after he took over Dragan's surgery yesterday afternoon.' Kate laughed. 'I see you didn't take up his offer to help out this morning, Nick.'

'I thought he'd suffered enough,' the senior partner said with a rare smile, 'though I have to say, with Dragan shortly going on paternity leave, I wish Dr Devereux was arriving sooner.'

'We'll manage, boss,' Oliver declared, and Nick's smile widened.

'I'll hold you to that.'

'Where is Tom this morning?' Chloe asked, and to Eve's dismay all eyes in Nick's consulting room turned to her.

'I don't know,' she said uncomfortably. 'He got a call this morning at breakfast, and I haven't seen him since.'

A breakfast that had been eaten in a strained, awkward silence with neither of them saying anything. A breakfast she'd eaten at breakneck speed, all too aware he was watching her every move.

'Sorry to interrupt,' Hazel declared to Eve's relief as she appeared at Nick's consulting-room door, 'but Mrs Banks is here, Eve, and she'd like a word with you.'

'With me?' Eve said in surprise.

The practice manager nodded, and Eve glanced across at Nick.

'I don't think we have anything else to discuss, do we?' the senior partner said, and, when everyone shook their heads, he said, 'you'd better see what she wants, Eve.'

Eve thought she'd better, too, though she couldn't imagine what Mrs Banks might want to talk to her about unless it was how Sophie was getting on in hospital.

It wasn't.

'I simply had to come in and thank you personally, Nurse,' Mrs Banks declared the minute she sat down in Eve's examination room. 'Dr Tremayne told me what you did for my Sophie, how she probably wouldn't have survived if it hadn't been for you, and I'll never forget it.'

'It's not me you should be thanking, Mrs Banks,' Eve replied with a smile. 'Dr Cornish, and his pilot, Michael Flannery, were the real heroes of the hour.'

'Yes, but they get paid to rescue people, you don't,' Sophie's mother said dismissively.

Eve stared, open-mouthed, at the woman sitting opposite her, then straightened in her seat.

'Dr Cornish and Michael Flannery may—as you say—be paid for the job they do,' she said, fighting to control her mounting anger with difficulty, 'but there are precious few people in the world who would be willing to put their own lives on the line every time they go into work. It takes a very special man—or woman—to join a rescue service, Mrs Banks.'

'Granted,' Sophie's mother observed, 'but Dr Cornish… Well, he always was a bit wild, reckless, and as for his father—'

'I'm afraid you'll have to excuse me,' Eve interrupted, getting abruptly to her feet and pointedly walking over to her examination-room door and opening it. 'I'm on a tight schedule this morning.'

She wasn't. In truth, she was actually finished for the day, but she knew if she sat in the same room as Mrs Banks for even a minute longer she wouldn't be responsible for her actions.

'Oh—of course,' Mrs Banks declared uncertainly. 'I know how busy you professionals are, but I felt I couldn't let another day go past without thanking you.'

Eve wished Sophie's mother hadn't said anything at all as the woman left.

How could Mrs Banks be so blinkered, so stupid? she wondered. Tom and Mitch might be paid for their work, but how could that possibly make their actions less courageous, less admirable?

She shook her head as she began gathering up the folders on her desk. And to think this was the village Tom had said he would be prepared to come back and live in. A village where people would never let him forget his origins or his youthful behaviour. He must have been insane.

*Or very deeply in love with you*, her heart whispered, and she bit her lip.

Part of her desperately wanted to believe he'd meant what he'd said. Part of her wondered if perhaps, this time, they might both be able to get it right, but she knew the part that wondered was her heart. Her heart which had deceived her all those years ago, telling he would change his mind, and stay in Penhally instead of going to the US, so she mustn't listen to it, she told herself as she picked up the last folder and strode down to

Reception to find Amanda Lovelace deep in conversation with their practice manager. This time she had to listen to her head. This time she had to be sensible because if it all went wrong again she knew she would never recover.

'Hello, there, Amanda,' she said, forcing a smile to her lips. 'I hope this isn't a medical visit?'

'Not at all,' Tassie's mother replied. 'Hazel loaned me a little portable gas stove to cook on while the electricity was off, and now it's back on again I thought I'd better return it.'

'How's Tassie?' Eve asked. 'None the worse, I hope, for her adventure?'

'She's fine. And talking about Tassie,' Amanda continued, steering Eve away from the reception desk, 'I just want to say thank you. Thank you *so* much.'

'For what?' Eve said in confusion, and Tassie's mother tapped the side of her nose and winked.

'You don't have to pretend, Eve. I have to say I wasn't very happy when Dr Cornish first suggested it—felt I couldn't be beholden—and I know he doesn't want thanks, or for anyone to know—he was most insistent about that—but I had to thank you because I'm guessing you came up with the idea.'

'Amanda, I don't know what—'

'I have to go,' Tassie's mother interrupted. 'I heard on the way down here that there might be a delivery of bread today at the corner shop, and you can bet your life it will all be sold out in ten minutes.'

'But, Amanda...'

She was too late. After giving her a big hug, Tassie's mother bustled away, leaving Eve standing in the centre of the waiting room with a puzzled frown. A frown that deepened when Tom strode through the surgery door.

'Whatever it was, I didn't do it.' He grinned as he saw her expression.

'You obviously did something,' she observed, 'because I have just had the weirdest conversation with Amanda Lovelace.'

'Ah,' he said.

'Yes, "ah".' She nodded. 'Care to elaborate?'

'Nothing to elaborate on,' he replied lightly but when she saw a tell-tale wash of embarrassed colour begin to creep across his cheeks, she folded her arms across her chest.

'Tom, you have two choices. Either you tell me what you've done, and how it involves Amanda, or I'll go round to her house this afternoon and ask her myself.'

He sighed, then guided her towards the waiting-room chairs furthest away from the reception desk.

'You know how you and Gertie are very keen for Tassie to apply for a scholarship to go to the Lady Joan Mercer's Boarding School in Devon?' he said.

'And you're dead against it,' Eve replied.

'Not against it,' he countered. 'Just worried about the possible long-term consequences for Tassie and her family. Well, I've been making discreet enquiries about Penhally High School, and it seems to be as good a school as it was in our day.'

'And?' Eve prompted.

'I've arranged with Mrs Lovelace to pay her a monthly allowance so she can afford to allow Tassie to stay on at the local school for as long as she wants.'

Eve's mouth opened and closed soundlessly, and she finally found her voice.

'But…' She paused and started again. 'Why would you want to do that?'

'Why not?' he countered.

'Well, for a start, you don't know Tassie, or her family,' she pointed out, and he shrugged.

'No, but I do know you, and if you think the child deserves help, then that's good enough for me.'

'But, Tom, have you considered the cost?' she protested. 'If Tassie stays on at school until she's eighteen, you'll be paying for her education for the next eight years.'

'A bit longer, probably,' he said, the colour on his cheeks darkening, 'because I said I'd keep paying if she wants to go to university. Look, I can afford it,' he continued as Eve tried to interrupt. 'It's no big deal.'

But it was, she thought. It was rather a large deal, and a sudden suspicion crept into her mind.

'When did you suggest this to Amanda?' she demanded.

'Yesterday morning.' He shot her a cool look. 'Long before I told you how I feel about you so this is not, in any shape or form, a bribe, Eve.'

In truth, that had been exactly what she'd been thinking, and she felt her cheeks redden.

'I'm sorry,' she murmured. 'I deserved that.'

'Yes, you did.'

She glanced at him hesitantly.

'It's very generous of you, Tom. More than generous, in fact, though I don't know how you managed to get Amanda to agree. She may not have much money, but she's a proud woman, and I would have thought she'd have considered it charity.'

'She did at first,' Tom admitted, 'but I talked her round.'

Eve's lips curved. 'In other words, you used the famous Tom Cornish charm. Well, I suppose it's never failed you yet.'

'Yes, it has,' he said, a wry smile appearing in his green eyes. 'With one very important person.'

'Tom…'

'I won't give up, you know.'

She opened her mouth to tell him she wished he would, but she didn't get the chance to say the words. The surgery door had opened with a bang, and Dragan stood there looking dishevelled, exhausted and absolutely elated.

'I have a son!' he exclaimed. 'I have a beautiful son, and

Melinda—she was terrific—much calmer than I was—and I…'
The smile on his face widened. 'I just had to come and tell you
all.'

Hazel let out a shriek of delight, and within seconds every
member of the Penhally practice had converged on the waiting
room.

'What weight is the baby?' Kate asked, as Nick pulled the
cork out of a bottle of champagne, and began filling some
glasses.

Dragan looked comically dismayed.

'I've no idea. The midwife did tell me, but I was just so
relieved my son had arrived safely, with the correct number of
fingers and toes, I didn't take it in.'

'Have you and Melinda decided on a name?' Chloe asked,
taking the glass of champagne Nick was holding out to her, and
the Croatian doctor shook his head.

'We didn't decide on a name or buy any baby clothes either,
or a cot,' he replied. 'We felt we might be somehow tempting
the gods if we did.'

'Then you'd better start hitting the shops in Truro fast.' Eve
laughed. 'New mums and babies are lucky if they're kept in
hospital for forty-eight hours these days.'

'I hadn't thought of that,' Dragan said, aghast. 'You're right,
I'd better go shopping right away.'

'But not until we've all toasted the new arrival,' Nick said.
'I always keep a bottle of champagne in the surgery for special
moments, and I think the birth of Melinda and Dragan's son certainly qualifies as one of those.'

'Hear! Hear!' Oliver called, and everyone laughed.

'Does everyone have a glass of champagne?' Nick asked,
and, when a chorus of assent rang out, he said, 'Then I want
you all to raise your glasses to the new arrival. May he have a
long and happy life, and have inherited his mother's looks,
and—' he winked across at Dragan '—his mother's brains, too.'

More laughter rippled round the room and, as everyone raised their glasses, Tom leant closer to Eve.

'Are you OK?' he murmured so low nobody else could hear him. 'I mean, if you'd rather not be here I can cover for you.'

She looked up at him, both surprised and touched he would realise occasions like this could be painful for her, and shook her head.

'I'm fine,' she said. 'Dragan… He had so little sunshine in his life until he met Melinda, and he deserves to be happy.'

'Eve…'

'Shush,' she whispered. 'I don't think Nick's finished yet.'

'Nick could talk for Cornwall,' Tom muttered, and Eve choked over her champagne, and waved an admonishing hand at him.

'I would also like to take this opportunity to say these last few days have been very difficult for everyone,' the senior partner continued. 'We've been through the kind of flood I never want to see again in my lifetime, and lost some good, decent people, but… But,' Nick added with emphasis, 'in the middle of the catastrophe my staff rose to the occasion magnificently, and I just want to thank you all, and say you were incredible.'

'You were pretty wonderful yourself, boss,' Oliver observed. 'Managing to assist at a breech birth with no electricity, and damn few medical instruments, takes some doing.'

A chorus of agreement met that comment, and Nick's cheeks flushed slightly, then he held up his hand, clearly calling for silence again.

'There is, however, one person who deserves my very special thanks,' he said. 'One person who I admit I have not made welcome since he came back to the village, and yet it is that one person without whose help things would most certainly have been considerably worse, so can I ask you to raise your glasses once more, and drink a toast to Tom Cornish? Penhally's very own, home-grown hero.'

'Tom Cornish!' everyone exclaimed, but when the toast had been drunk and Dragan was, yet again, being bombarded with more questions about his son, Tom looked down at Eve quizzically.

'Did you know he was going to say that?' he asked.

'I'm as surprised as you are,' she replied. 'Considering how unfriendly he's been towards you since you came back, I'd have thought you were the last person he would have wanted to thank.'

And not just thank, Eve discovered as Nick eased his way through the throng towards them, with Kate at his side.

'I owe you an apology,' the senior partner declared the moment he drew level with Tom.

'Forget it, Nick,' Tom said, and Nick shook his head.

'I can't,' he declared. 'I know I have a brusque tongue—'

'You can say that again,' Kate murmured, and Nick gave her a hard stare.

'And sometimes speak before I think,' the senior partner continued, 'but I will be eternally grateful for everything you did for the village. If you hadn't been here, I don't know what would have happened.'

'I just wish there could have been no fatalities,' Tom observed. 'Reverend Kenner seems to have been a well-liked man, and Mrs Baxter… She and I may not have seen eye to eye, but I'm sorry she's dead.'

'Did you know that Lauren is giving Foxy a home?' Kate said as Nick walked away in answer to Oliver's beckoning wave. 'The dog knows her, you see, from when she used to do Audrey's physio, so he's not scared of her, and she actually got him to eat something yesterday which the RSPCA says is a miracle because he's point-blank refused to take food from anybody else.'

'I just wish we could find Chloe's cats,' Tom declared,

glancing across to where the midwife was talking animatedly to Dragan. 'But there's no sign of them—not even their bodies. In fact, I was wondering—'

'Tom, I think Mitch wants a word with you,' Eve interrupted, seeing the redheaded pilot hovering in the waiting-room doorway pointing silently at Tom and then at himself.

'I'll be back in a minute,' Tom said, half turning to go, then he stopped. 'Don't go anywhere. Stay here.'

'Yes, sir.' Eve laughed.

But he was going somewhere, she thought, feeling her smile slip sideways when Tom reached Mitch and the pilot ruefully handed him a sheaf of papers.

They were leaving. She could see it in Tom's face. Mitch must have received a fax from their headquarters, and they were leaving.

Well, she'd known it was going to happen eventually, she thought as she took a sip of champagne then put her glass down. She'd just hoped—stupidly—that he might have been able to stay for a few more days.

'What's up?' Kate asked, gesturing towards Mitch and Tom.

'I think Tom's just received a call from Deltaron,' Eve replied.

'But that means he'll be leaving,' Kate said with dismay, and Eve forced a smile to her lips.

'He was never going to stay, Kate. His work—his life— isn't here.'

'But I thought…'

Eve didn't give the midwife the chance to tell her what she'd thought. Instead, she made her way towards Oliver, Lauren and Chloe who were standing by the window.

'Isn't it marvellous news?' Lauren beamed when she saw her. 'Melinda and Dragan must be so happy.'

'Christenings and weddings.' Chloe laughed. 'Reverend Kenner is going to be…' She came to an abrupt halt, and bit her lip. 'Sorry. Force of habit. It's so hard to believe he's gone, isn't it?'

'How is Rachel?' Eve asked. 'I thought I might call in on her this afternoon, see how she is.'

'She's gone to Plymouth with her aunt and uncle,' Lauren replied. 'She'll come back for the funeral, of course, but I think she wanted out of the village with all its memories.'

'She's a very brave girl—braver than I would be in the circumstances,' Chloe observed. 'To be left with no mother, no father, and expecting a baby… It's going to be tough for her.'

'She'll cope,' Eve said, her eyes following Tom as he scanned the waiting room, clearly looking for her. 'We all have to cope in different ways with what life throws at us, and she'll cope.'

'I thought I told you to stay where you were,' Tom declared with a frown when he reached her side. 'Give a woman a simple order, and what does she do? Completely ignores it.'

'I can see why you've never married, Tom.' Chloe laughed, and he gazed at her severely.

'You know, for that remark, I should refuse to give you the present one of my men has just brought in for you.'

'What present?' she said, looking puzzled.

'Actually, I'm more interested in meeting the bloke who thinks he can give my fiancée presents,' Oliver said, his voice mock stern, and Tom grinned.

'It's two presents actually,' he said. 'One is ginger and has only one eye, and one is white with a black patch over its eye.'

'You've found Cyclops and Pirate?' Chloe gasped, her face lighting up.

'One of my men has. They're outside in cat boxes if you want to see for yourself.'

Chloe was already halfway out of the room, and Oliver gripped Tom's hand fervently.

'Thanks, mate,' he said. 'I owe you. I owe you big time.'

'Are you sure your name isn't actually Santa Claus?' Eve said when the couple had gone, and Tom laughed.

'I didn't find them—Gregory did. He thinks they must have

decided to take shelter on top of one of the wardrobes because they weren't even a little bit dirty or wet.'

'Lucky cats,' Eve observed.

'Eve…'

He cleared his throat, and she knew what was coming. He was going to tell her he was leaving. She could see it in his face, and she didn't want to say goodbye to him. She'd said it to him once before, and she didn't want to say it again.

'I think Nick is trying to attract your attention,' she said quickly, and, when Tom groaned, she nudged him firmly with her hand. 'Look, if he wants to thank you again, just smile and accept it with good grace.'

He went reluctantly, and she waited only until he was deep in conversation with the senior partner then quietly slipped out of the surgery. He would be angry—perhaps even upset—when he found out she had gone, but she'd much rather he just disappeared out of her life as silently as he'd reappeared in it. To say goodbye to him, knowing she would never see him again… She didn't have that much courage.

'Lovely day, isn't it?' a woman called from outside one of the shops as Eve walked quickly past.

'Beautiful, yes,' Eve managed to reply.

'You and your gentleman friend must come back once we've redecorated,' the woman continued. 'You never did get your lemon meringue pies.'

It was the woman from the café, and Eve should have recognised her immediately but she hadn't.

'We'll do that,' she said, but of course they wouldn't.

By this time tomorrow Tom would be somewhere overseas, and she would have her work, and Tassie, to fill her days, and maybe, in time, she might forget this brief interlude. Though never completely, she thought as she crossed Harbour Bridge, and heard the chug of the firemen's hoses as they continued to pump water out of the houses. No matter how hard she tried, the day of the flood would be forever etched on her memory, whether she wanted it to be or not.

But she would survive, she told herself as she headed towards the lighthouse. She had survived before, and she would survive again.

'Kate, have you seen Eve anywhere?' Tom said with a frown as he walked towards her.

'She's gone, Tom,' the midwife replied. 'While you were talking to Nick she just slipped away. I imagine she's gone home.'

'Not home, no,' Tom said thoughtfully, 'but I think I might know where she is.'

He turned to leave, and Kate put her hand out to stay him.

'I hear you're off on another mission?' she said, and he nodded.

'Earthquake in China. We're flying out tonight, but I need to return to Switzerland first to finalise a team.'

'You be careful, you hear?' Kate declared, and he grinned.

'Hey, I'm always careful,' he said, and she shook her head.

'I don't mean in China. I mean with Eve.' On impulse, Kate stood on her toes and kissed him lightly on the cheek. 'That's for luck,' she whispered, 'and now go after her.'

'You'll make my apologies to the others?' he said.

'Of course, I will,' the midwife said. 'Now, *go*.'

He did.

'First Eve disappears, then Tom,' Nick declared when he joined Kate. 'What's going on between that pair? Are they an item again, or what?'

'I think whatever Tom says to her when he finds her will decide what their futures are going to be,' Kate murmured.

The senior partner frowned as stared down at her.

'I'm sorry, but you've lost me.'

Kate smiled.

'Let's just keep your fingers crossed for them, Nick. They both deserve to be happy, and that was a very nice apology you made to Tom.'

'Well, I had to give credit where credit was due,' Nick replied, 'and I think I was wrong about him.'

'I think you were, too,' Kate replied, but as she made to move away Nick caught her by the elbow.

'Kate, on the night of the flood…' He looked uncomfortable, ill at ease, then he firmed his jaw. 'What you said—about Jem. I can't make you any promises, but I will try.'

She looked up at him, her eyes very bright, then nodded.

'That's all I want, Nick,' she said, her voice husky. 'It's all I've ever wanted.'

She should have brought her jacket, Eve thought as she sat on the grass below the lighthouse, and hugged her knees. She was wearing her cherry-red sweater and a heavy tweed skirt, but there was no denying that autumn had well and truly arrived. There was a chill in the air, a feeling of darker nights approaching, and the scent of dried leaves now mingled with the tang of seaweed.

'I could see you shivering from all the way back at the church.'

Eve glanced over her shoulder to see Tom standing behind her, and sighed. She might have known she wouldn't be able to get away from him so easily.

'How did you know I would be here?' she asked as he took off his jacket, and put it round her shoulders before she could prevent him.

'No great mystery,' he said. 'I knew you would want to think, and this is where you always used to come if you had a problem.'

'It's amazing how many unimportant things you seem to remember about me,' she replied.

'I remember everything about you—I told you that.'

She gazed back out at the sea.

'Water… It's so very beautiful isn't it?' she said. 'And yet it can be so cruel and deadly, too.'

He sat down beside her on the grass.

'Mankind thinks itself so smart, so clever,' he said, 'but it's Nature that wields the real power. It can be a horrifying power at times, a terrifying power, but Nature also has the ability to heal. I've seen whole forests reduced to a smoking ruin and yet, within a year, wildflowers will have appeared, and the first shoots of new trees.'

She picked at the grass beside her for a few moments, then took a deep breath.

'How soon are you leaving?'

'I should be on my way now, but I didn't want to leave without saying goodbye.'

She stared down at the grass again, knowing that if she turned her head slightly she would see all of Penhally Bay spread out before her. The lifeboat station, St Mark's on the hill, the houses clustered round the harbour, and the newer bungalows higher on the hill. Everything would look just the same, but not quite the same any more, and it never would be because of the man sitting beside her.

'Have you decided what you're going to do?' she asked. 'I mean, are you staying with Deltaron, or…'

'I think you're right, that Deltaron is where I'm supposed to be,' he replied, 'but only if…'

She waited for him to finish, but when he didn't she turned to face him.

'If what, Tom?'

'Before I answer that question, I have something to give you. I bought…' Awkwardly he held out the plastic carrier bag he was clutching. 'I don't know whether this will help, or if I've got this wrong again, but I was thinking about what you said yesterday, and I thought… But maybe it's not a good idea, maybe you might think…'

'Tom, what are you trying to say?' she demanded, and when for an answer he produced a small nosegay of flowers from his bag she stared at them blankly. 'You bought me flowers?'

'I bought them for her,' he said, his voice half-muffled, his head lowered as though he was afraid to meet her eyes. 'For our daughter. You said yesterday that what upset you most was there being no grave, nowhere you could go and say you were sorry. Well, I want…' She saw him swallow. 'I want to tell her I'm sorry, too. Sorry for letting her mother down, for not being there for her when she needed me.'

'Tom—'

'Eve, I want our baby to know I'm thinking of her, and I thought…' His head came up, and when his eyes met hers she saw the pain and anguish she knew were in her own eyes mirrored in his. 'I thought maybe I could put this in the sea— if you wouldn't mind if I did that—in in memory of her.'

Tears began to trickle down her cheeks and into her mouth.

'You really want to do that?' she said, scarcely able to see him through her tears.

'She was my baby, too, Eve. My daughter, too, and maybe…' His voice broke. 'Maybe…if I do this she might know that though she's not here with me—with us—we will never forget her, and we will always, always love her.'

'Tom… I…'

Eve couldn't say another word and when he hesitantly, awkwardly, held out his arms to her, she reached for him, too, and clung to him and felt him shudder, and knew he was crying as much as she was for the child they might have had and who they would never forget.

And, when they were calmer, they walked together to the headland, and threw the little nosegay Tom had bought up into the air, watched it soar for a few seconds, a myriad of bright colours in the blue sky, then land with a gentle splash in the water, and clung to one another again and cried again.

'I know this is too soon,' Tom said with difficulty when their grief was spent. 'So much has happened—and you're fragile right now—and I…I'm pretty shaky myself—but do you think—is there any possibility—that we might start again?'

'I don't know, Tom,' she said uncertainly. 'We have so much history. Maybe too much.'

'You said…' He caught her hands, and held them tightly. 'When you first told me about the baby—you said you loved me all those years ago. Has it all gone—that love?'

'I think…' She stared up into the face she knew so well, at the lines which seemed to have become even more deeply etched around his eyes and on his forehead over the past few days. 'I think I will always love you, Tom, but I don't know whether loving you would be enough. What happened—the baby—I think it might always come between us. Not spoken about, but always there, and when we argued—and we would argue because all couples do— my fear is we'd use it as a weapon against one another.'

'I wouldn't.'

She smiled unevenly.

'You can't be sure of that, Tom.'

'Eve, no one can be sure of anything,' he insisted. 'We might have years of happiness together, or our lives could be snuffed out in a second by some pointless car crash. You said I wasn't to blame for Charlie's death, and for the deaths of those people in India, because I did what I thought was right at the time— that it was all anyone could do. Well, the decision you made about the baby was right for you at the time, it was all *you* could do, and you have to see that, accept that.'

'I hear what you're saying, Tom,' she murmured, 'and my head tells me you're right, but my heart…'

'Eve, I have loved you for so long,' he said, his voice constricted. 'I was in love with you even when we were at school.'

'No, you weren't,' she said. 'Starchy Dwyer, remember?'

'Do you want to know why I called you that?' he said. 'It was because I fancied you like mad but I was the no-hoper, Tom Cornish's son, whereas you... You were the one who always got the good grades, the one whose parents were respectable, acceptable, and I'd have looked a proper fool in front of my friends if I'd asked you out, and you'd said no, so it was easier to act like I thought you were the prat.'

'It was a pretty good act,' she said with feeling, and his lips curved into a slight smile, then the smile disappeared.

'Eve, I want to spend the rest of my life with you. Yes, we've made mistakes, and I made the biggest one of all, but I need you, Eve. It's not just the wanting—though God knows I want you so much—but...' He let go of her hands and thrust his fingers through his hair, his face taut, strained. 'I *need* you.'

'Tom—'

'No, please, let me finish,' he pressed. 'All these years I've been chasing dreams, and nothing brought me any happiness, any contentment, because you weren't in my life. When I think of all the years we could have had together, the memories we could have made and shared. I lost them. Me. Not you. Me, always on the move, thinking excitement was the answer, when all the time what I really wanted was here, in my own back yard, because, you see...' His voice cracked. 'You are my dreams, Eve, you always have been.'

There was honesty and truth in his face, and she knew she would never love anyone as much as she loved him, but so much had happened over the last few days, and she felt raw, exposed, vulnerable.

'Twenty years, Tom,' she said slowly. 'It's a lot of years to forget.'

'I'm not asking you to forget them,' he said, his voice soft with understanding. 'I know you can't, just as I know I can't go back and give myself the knowledge I have now. I wish I could. I wish I hadn't been the stupid, blind, selfish person I was then, but all the wishing in the world can't make that happen, but if we can both—somehow—forgive ourselves, then maybe we won't just have a shared past. Maybe we can have a future, together.'

'But, you're leaving,' she said. 'You're going to China.'

'Yes, I'm leaving.' He nodded. 'But what I want to know is, if I come back to Penhally, when all of this upheaval is over, would you want to see me again?'

She gazed out to sea to where the little nosegay was floating away towards the horizon, and then she looked up at him. Up into the face that had once haunted her dreams, the face she'd once loved, and then hated, and saw the entreaty in his eyes, the desperate hope, and though she didn't know what the future was going to bring she did know that the fates had given her another chance at happiness and she would be foolish to let it go.

'Yes,' she said, her voice a little wobbly, a little tremulous. 'I'd want to see you again, Tom.'

And a blinding smile illuminated his face, and he caught her hand, and pressed her knuckles to his lips.

'One day at a time, Eve,' he said. 'We'll take this one day at a time, and no matter how long it takes I will wait for you.'

And she smiled back at him, and nodded, and together they walked back down into Penhally Bay.

# EPILOGUE

*Six months later*

DUSK. A magical time, a perfect time for a wedding. That's what any guest staying at the exclusive Lake Lausanne hotel would have said if they'd looked out of the dining-room windows onto the lawn and seen a clergyman and two other men standing beside an archway of spring blossom, clearly waiting for a bride to arrive. However, if those guests had looked a little closer, they would have seen that one of the men looked distinctly nervous.

'Mitch, are you quite sure this morning suit doesn't make me look like a complete prat?'

'Well, now you come to mention it…' the pilot began, then grinned as Tom gazed at him in dismay. 'You look fine.'

Tom tugged at his tie. 'Shouldn't Eve be here by now?'

'Tom, Eve is not going to do a runner, although I will if you keep on stressing.'

'Right. Sorry,' Tom muttered, glancing down at his watch.

'Eight minutes,' Mitch observed.

'What?'

'The ceremony is due to begin in eight minutes,' the pilot declared. 'Which is exactly two minutes less than the time was when you last checked your watch.'

'Right.'

Mitch shot Tom a mischievous glance.

'Wouldn't it just be typical if we were to get a call from Deltaron?' he said, then guffawed when Tom's mouth fell open in horror. 'Just kidding. They know you're not available. Know I'm not, too. No way was I going to miss out on being your best man.'

'I really appreciate you agreeing to do this, Mitch,' Tom said awkwardly. 'It's…well…it's very good of you.'

The big pilot looked equally embarrassed.

'Me miss out on the opportunity of seeing the head of operations at Deltaron in a complete panic? No chance.'

'I guess not.' Tom smiled, then glanced down at his watch again.

'Seven minutes,' Mitch said, 'and if you look at your watch one more time I'll ram it down your throat.'

'Amanda, are you sure we're not late?' Eve said as she glanced out of the French windows of the hotel. 'Tom's walking up and down out there like he's scared I'm not going to turn up or something.'

'Of course you're not late,' Amanda insisted as Tassie pirouetted past them, clearly revelling in her pale blue bridesmaid's dress. 'And, even if you were, it's the bride's prerogative.'

'Not this bride,' Eve said with a shaky laugh. 'This bride's been waiting twenty years for this moment.'

'No doubts, then?' Tassie's mother said, and Eve shook her head.

'None at all,' she replied, and she didn't have, not now.

Bit by bit, over the last six months, Tom had chipped away at her worries, emailing or phoning her every day, but it was when he had returned to Penhally for both Melinda and Rachel's little boys' christenings that she had finally been convinced. She knew he would never feel comfortable in Penhally, and yet he'd come back because she'd wanted him to. Come back to make her happy, and it was that which convinced her to say yes when he'd asked her to marry him, and that night, after Rachel's baby's christening...

Her face softened. She'd been so nervous and self-conscious that night, and he'd been so gentle, so tender, making her laugh, relaxing her, so their joining had been even more wonderful, even more perfect, than it had been the last time they'd made love twenty years ago.

'I still can't believe you're actually going to be living here,' Amanda continued. 'I thought you were like me—destined always to stay in Penhally.'

'I thought so, too,' Eve admitted, 'but it makes sense for us to live in Switzerland when most of Tom's team have homes here, and...' She shrugged. 'I think it's maybe way past time I spread my wings.'

'Tassie and I wouldn't be here at all if Tom hadn't paid our air fares,' Amanda said. 'We owe you so—'

'You owe us nothing,' Eve interrupted, putting her fingers to the woman's lips quickly to silence her. 'We wanted you at our wedding, and I'll be very cross if you don't use those other air tickets Tom gave you to come and visit us regularly.'

'But—'

'No buts,' Eve insisted. 'Tassie's special, and so are you.'

'I don't know about us being special,' Amanda said, blowing her nose vigorously, 'but you certainly look lovely today. That colour really suits you.'

Eve uncertainly smoothed down the folds of the long crimson skirt and matching embroidered bolero jacket she was wearing.

'You don't think it looks odd, me wearing red?' she said. 'It's just Tom likes this colour—'

'I think you look gorgeous,' Amanda insisted. 'Like you have a candle inside you, burning with happiness.'

It was how Eve felt as she stepped out of the French windows and saw Mitch nudge Tom, and Tom's whole face light up when he turned and saw her. It was how she felt throughout the whole ceremony as Tom repeated his vows, his voice a little husky, and she made her own pledges, her voice just as uneven, and his fingers tightened round hers as though he never wanted to let her go.

She didn't want to let go of him either. All she wanted was to be alone with him, but Mitch had organised a wedding supper for them and she knew it would have seemed ungrateful if she and Tom had slipped away the minute they'd finished eating.

Mitch obviously didn't agree. In fact, the second their plates were cleared, the pilot gave Amanda a very decided wink, then glanced at his watch.

'Half past nine already,' he said. 'I think it's time some folk should be in their beds.'

'But I don't normally go to bed until ten o'clock,' Tassie protested and, as Amanda laughed, and Eve blushed, Tom got to his feet.

'I couldn't agree with you more, Mitch,' he said, 'but there's something I want to do first.'

Eve's eyebrows rose as he strode across to the quartet who had been playing a medley of tunes throughout the evening.

'What he's up to, Mitch?' she asked and the pilot shook his head.

'Haven't a clue, love.'

Neither did she until the quartet began to play the opening bars of a tune she recognised instantly, and when Tom held out his arms to her, she had to blink very rapidly before she could walk out onto the small dance floor and join him.

'My very own Lady in Red,' he murmured into her hair as he drew her into his arms. 'And you are mine now, for always, aren't you?'

And she was, she thought as he whirled her round the small dance floor, holding her closer, and closer, moulding his body to hers, so she could feel the uneven throb of his heartbeat, could see his eyes growing darker and more intense with every passing second and, when the music ended, and he kissed her, she never wanted the kiss to end.

Neither, it seemed, did the other diners if the eruption of applause, and the sound of Mitch whooping enthusiastically, was anything to go by when they finally drew apart.

'I think maybe Mitch was right,' Tom said, leaning his forehead against hers, his cheeks flushed, his breathing uneven. 'Maybe it *is* time we go to bed before I completely forget we're not alone.'

'Definitely,' she said, chuckling shakily as the leader of the quartet shook her hand, and said something incomprehensible in Swiss, and the diners applauded again.

She thought it even more when Tom drew her back into his arms the second they reached their hotel room.

'Oh, Tom, I am so happy.' She sighed, as he slid his hands up her sides so she felt the heat of his fingers through the fine satin of her jacket. 'I keep thinking I'm going to wake up, find this is all a dream, that no one has the right to be as happy as I am right now.'

'You do,' he said, tracing the outline of her jaw with his lips. 'You deserve everything you've ever wanted, and I'm going to make it my life's ambition to ensure you get it.'

'You already have,' she said huskily. 'In fact…' She took a deep breath. 'There's something I have to tell you.'

'Later,' he said, his eyes liquid with desire as he began unbuttoning her jacket. 'Later we talk, but right now…'

She wanted the 'right now', too, she thought as he eased her jacket off, then her bra, and when he caressed her breasts with his fingers and lips she felt the heat flare everywhere. Every part of her body seemed so much more sensitive tonight, she thought as he removed the rest of her clothing, then his, and she knew why but it would keep. Just for a little while it would keep, she decided as she clung to him, revelling in his hardness as he whispered words of love, and touched her, and kissed her, telling her over and over how beautiful she was, how desirable, until she was shaking with need.

'Tom, please—*please*,' she gasped, wanting more, even more.

And he laughed, and kissed her again, and just when she thought she wouldn't be able to bear it any longer, he finally entered her, hot and slick, and she rose up to join him, wanting to give him the same joy he was giving her, and felt her heart clutch with happiness when he carried her over the edge and his cry matched hers as they spiralled and shuddered and climaxed together.

'My wife,' he said, gathering her, spoon-like, against his chest. 'You're all I've ever wanted Eve, all I'll ever need.'

She gazed down at his arms encircling her, and cleared her throat.

'Tom…do you remember when you told me how much you would like to have children?'

His grip on her tightened.

'Eve, I'm happy simply having you,' he said softly. 'I'm not saying it wouldn't be a great joy to me if we were so blessed, but…' He turned her round in his arms so he could look at her. 'For such a long time I thought I'd lost you. For an even longer time I thought I'd messed things up completely. If we should have a baby then it would be wonderful because you deserve so much to be a mother, but if we're not lucky—if it doesn't happen— you've already made my life complete, just by being you.'

'You've made my life complete, too,' she said unevenly, 'but what I meant…' She could feel her cheeks darkening which was ridiculous because she had nothing to feel embarrassed about, but she so wanted him to feel the same way she did. 'When I asked whether you still wanted to be a father I was thinking of… perhaps in about six months?'

'Six months?' he repeated with a frown. 'Eve—'

'Tom, when did we first make love again?' she interrupted, and saw his frown deepen.

'It was when I came back for Rachel's son's christening. When I asked you to marry me, and you…' He smiled. 'You said yes, and made me the happiest man on the planet.'

'That was three months ago, Tom.' He still looked confused and she chuckled softly. 'And you call yourself a doctor. Think about it. Tom. If I'm asking whether you would like to be a father in six months' time, and we made love three months ago…'

He stared at her silently for a second, then sat up so fast she had to catch hold of him to prevent herself landing face down in the pillow.

'You're pregnant?' He gasped.

'Yes.' She nodded, watching his face anxiously.

A smile tugged at his lips. A smile that grew, and grew, and tentatively he reached out and gently put his fingers on her stomach.

'A baby,' he said, wonder plain in his voice. 'We're going to have a baby.'

'Are…are you pleased?' she said, and he dashed his hand across his eyes.

'Oh, Eve,' he said, his voice husky. 'Oh, my love, my *love*.'

And he clasped her to him, his eyes as bright and shimmering as she knew hers must be, then released her abruptly, concern plain on his face, and gently touched her tummy again, and she laughed, a hiccuping laugh that was halfway towards a sob.

'Tom, I'm not made of glass,' she said. 'I won't break.'

'No, but I think I might,' he said. 'Break with happiness, and joy.'

And he drew her to him again and kissed her so tenderly, and she felt the wetness on his cheeks, knew her own cheeks were tear-stained, too, but they were tears of happiness. That at last—at long last—she and Tom would have not just a past together, but a glorious, wonderful future.

**\* \* \* \***

# BRIDES OF PENHALLY BAY

*Let us whisk you away to this Cornish coastal town – to a place where hearts are made whole.*

Read on for a sneak preview from
*Dr Devereux's Proposal* by Margaret McDonagh
– the twelfth book in the
BRIDES OF PENHALLY BAY series.

## DR DEVEREUX'S PROPOSAL
### by Margaret McDonagh

Shutting off the water, he stepped out of the cubicle and reached for a towel, hesitating when he heard a noise downstairs. It had sounded like the front door closing. Frowning, Gabriel waited, listening. Yes, there was definitely someone moving around inside the house. More curious than concerned, he wrapped the towel around his waist and left his bedroom, moving silently down the stairs to investigate the trespass into his new domain. The noises were louder now. He tiptoed in the direction from which they came, pausing in the shadows of the unlit passageway to look through the door into a large, homely farmhouse kitchen.

A brindle-and-white greyhound lay on the stone-flagged floor, its head on its paws, solemnly watching the movements of the woman who was moving about as if she owned the place. Guessing her age to be in the late twenties, Gabriel's gaze lingered on her with as much intensity as the dog's, warmth and pure masculine appreciation spearing through him, catching him by surprise.

A bunch of home-cut flowers, dahlias and chrysanthemums amongst them, were arranged haphazardly in an old stoneware jug on the table, while several carrier bags littered the polished wooden work surfaces. Humming an unrecognisable tune, the woman busied herself stocking the kitchen cupboards with her purchases, her movements athletically graceful. Tight white jeans accentuated the length of her legs and lovingly moulded the rounded swell of her derrière. As she turned round, still unaware of his presence, he could see how the super-soft angora jumper she wore skimmed her shapely frame, outlining the curves of full, firm breasts. The lavender colour set off the natural paler highlights in her light brown hair and lent an amethyst glow to what he could see, even from this distance, were gorgeous grey eyes. Gabriel was mesmerised. Who was this woman?

Picking up a carton of milk and a box of eggs, she twirled her way to the fridge on trainer-clad feet, presenting him with a delectable view of her feminine curves as she bent over, her hips swaying provocatively to the music she heard in her head. Left loose, her wavy hair cascaded round her shoulders in a darkly golden curtain. She flicked it back with one hand as she rose and returned to the counter, still humming to herself as she delved into the carrier bags once more.

Intrigued, Gabriel stepped into the room. The dog was the first to acknowledge him. Anxious brown eyes turned his way, then the too-thin creature whined and all but crawled towards the woman, who leaned down to stroke it with gentle care.

'What's wrong, Foxy?'

Knowing whatever he did was going to startle her, Gabriel cleared his throat, announcing his presence as he walked forward. 'Hello.'

With a shocked cry, the woman swung round, the pack of pasta shells in her hands dropping to the floor. Beautiful smoky grey eyes widened between long, dark lashes as she stared at him, and lushly kissable lips parted in surprise. Her tongue-tip peeped out to moisten them as she stepped back a pace, one hand dropping to calm the fretful dog pressed against her legs, the other curled to a fist at her throat. Gabriel felt her gaze skim over his scantily clad frame and an unexpected but immediate wave of attraction crashed through him.

'I'm sorry.' He offered a smile with the apology, unable to look away from her. 'I didn't mean to scare you. I heard a noise down here and had no idea anyone was around.'

'OK. Um…hello,' she greeted after a moment, her voice melodious but with a husky undertone that appealed to him. Hell, everything about her appealed to him. 'You must be Dr Devereux. I wasn't expecting you until tomorrow,' she continued, bending to pick up the fallen pasta, fumbling briefly as she set it awkwardly back on the counter. With a sudden smile that had the same effect on him as a punch to the solar plexus, she held out her hand. 'I'm Lauren Nightingale…your neighbour at Gatehouse Cottage and also physiotherapist at the Penhally Bay Surgery.'

*This* was the woman Nick Tremayne had spoken of? *Ooh la la!* 'Lauren, it is a pleasure to meet you. Please, call me Gabriel,' he invited, trying to pull himself together and remember his manners.

Closing the remaining gap between them, he took her graceful hand in his. Her grip was strong, her fingers slender but capable. Looking down, he noted how much paler her warm, satiny skin was than his, how her bones were far more delicate. A jolt of electricity zinged up his arm and along his nerve endings at the contact between them. That Lauren felt it, too, was apparent by the way she bit her lip, her pupils dilating, her body momentarily swaying towards him before she caught herself and pulled back, withdrawing her hand. Gabriel released her with reluctance.

Close to, she was taller than he had realised, five-seven or -eight, he judged, and even more attractive than he had first thought. She had an earthy allure quite unlike the sophisticated, deliberate beauty of some of the Parisian women he had dated in the past but vastly more entrancing and natural. A subtle, floral scent—sweet peas, he recognised  mingled with her unique femininity, teasing and enticing him. No make-up was needed to enhance her flawless skin. Pale gold from a fading summer tan, it looked as smooth as silk. His fingers longed to touch, to discover if she was as warm and soft all over as her hand had felt in his. He struggled to rein back the runaway thoughts but it wasn't easy when every particle of his being hummed with awareness while she studied him as closely as he had regarded her.

Dr Gabriel Devereux was the most delicious surprise!

Fearing that her legs would not hold her upright much

longer, Lauren leaned against the kitchen counter and affected what she hoped was a nonchalant pose. She didn't *feel* remotely nonchalant. Any minute now she was going to do something uncharacteristically shocking, impulsive and embarrassing…like throw herself wantonly into his arms and ravish him.

Gabriel's sudden arrival had taken her off guard. She was disconcerted that she had not been aware of his presence and wondered how long he had stood there watching her. But the fact that she had not seen him in the shadows and had only formed a distinct visual impression when he had stepped into the brightly lit kitchen stirred inner anxieties she was unwilling to deal with. That he was wearing only an ivory towel was a suitable diversion, however, and she grabbed the excuse to ignore her disturbing concerns, unable to resist the temptation to observe him in detail.

She saw bare bodies, or bits of bodies, every working day, but she had never seen one that made her heart hammer, her mouth water and that robbed her of breath as Gabriel's did. Goodness! Her hands clung to the counter as she greedily inspected him. She feared she was about to melt into a puddle at his feet. Nice feet, too, she couldn't help but notice. Very nice. Like the rest of him. Her gaze slowly climbed back up his scrumptious frame.

Strong, lean legs were braced hip-width apart and the towel slung low around his hips revealed a tantalising glimpse of pleasingly muscled, hair-brushed thighs. A narrow line of dark hair in the centre of his flat stomach dipped past his navel and disappeared below the towel. She licked her lips, resisting the urge to touch as she looked over his perfect athletic body, toned abdomen, well-defined chest and broad shoulders, all supple flesh and rippling muscle. He'd clearly just stepped out of the shower as droplets of water glistened on his delicious dark caramel skin, its colour hinting at a French

Caribbean ancestry. Lauren swallowed, battling against the overwhelming desire to press her lips to that warm, damp masculine flesh. She still remembered the faint scent of him when they had been close and shaken hands…tangy citrus soap and clean male, heady and earthy and arousing.

Topping six feet, he was more than impressive. The close-cropped dark hair suited him, accentuating the classically beautiful but supremely masculine bone structure of his face, the slash of high cheekbones, the straight nose and the carved lines of his jaw. Her palm itched to smooth over his head, to feel if the razor-short hair was rough or soft to the touch. His mouth was undeniably sexy, his bronze lips sensually curved and designed for kissing. She yearned to press her own against them, to learn the shape and feel and taste of him.

Twin dimples creased his cheeks when he smiled, while laughter lines fanned out from the corners of his eyes, adding character and hinting at an active sense of humour. Finally, she looked into those thickly lashed eyes. They were the richest brown she had ever seen. As Gabriel met and held her gaze, his pupils dilated, darkening the irises to the colour of finest coffee. The flare of masculine interest was unmistakable and caused a tightening ache of want in the pit of her stomach that was so strong and so sudden she barely suppressed a gasp.

What in the world had come over her?

# *Maggie Kingsley*
## QUESTIONS & ANSWERS

### Would you like to live in the fictional Cornish town of Penhally Bay?

Oddly enough my family and I lived in Cornwall when my sisters and I were small, so writing the book brought back a lot of happy memories for me. Picnics on the beach, my dad's ancient Austin car… It was thirty years old when he bought it, and the indicator lights were the old-fashioned sort which stuck out whenever he indicated right or left. Trouble was they would never go back in again so, on days out, we kids were deputised to hang out of the window and push them in!

### Did you enjoy writing as part of the Brides of Penhally Bay series?

Very much indeed. It was strange at first to be given the names of your hero and heroine, and a rough outline of the plot, but because we were also given complete flexibility we all very quickly made both our plots and central characters our own.

### What was it like working with other authors to create the backdrop to these books?

We had a lot of fun deciding which of the subsidiary characters we would kill off and who would be allowed to live. Writers are wicked, wicked people deep down!

## Tell us about a typical day's writing!

It varies. For example, if I've just started a new book I'll drink at least five cups of coffee and eat four slices of toast a day whilst staring blankly at my computer screen. If I'm in the middle of a book, the caffeine and toast intake escalates big time, and the staring at the computer becomes accompanied by many deep sighs and mutters of, 'This isn't working.' Once I've reached what I think of as the crest of the hill, writing-wise, I forget to eat or drink, and just type manically. Writers aren't just wicked, they're also seriously weird!

## How did you first start writing romance novels?

You want the truth about the 'how' rather than the 'why'? I'd always wanted to be a writer but I was – still am – a lousy typist and, because I only had an ancient typewriter, any rewrites took forever and my pages were still covered with Tippex. After I hurt my back, and became unemployed, I decided to do a long-distance computer course. The college gave me a computer to use in my own home, and once I'd discovered how to cut, paste, and delete, I began using the computer in the evenings to write stories. Without that computer I doubt I'd be where I am today and, if anyone from the college is reading this, I didn't start the course just to get the use of a free computer. Honestly, I didn't!

## What do you love most about your hero and heroine in *A Baby for Eve*?

That they're completely real people who deserve so much to be happy, but for a variety of reasons they're not. They get things wrong, screw things up, make – and have made – mistakes like everyone else, so when I finally got Tom and Eve together at the end of the book I had a huge smile on my face.

# 4 FREE

## BOOKS AND A SURPRISE GIFT!

We would like to take this opportunity to thank you for reading this Mills & Boon® book by offering you the chance to take FOUR more specially selected titles from the Medical™ series absolutely FREE! We're also making this offer to introduce you to the benefits of the Mills & Boon® Book Club—

- ★ **FREE home delivery**
- ★ **FREE gifts and competitions**
- ★ **FREE monthly Newsletter**
- ★ **Exclusive Mills & Boon® Book Club offers**
- ★ **Books available before they're in the shops**

Accepting these FREE books and gift places you under no obligation to buy, you may cancel at any time, even after receiving your free shipment. Simply complete your details below and return the entire page to the address below. You don't even need a stamp!

**YES!** Please send me 4 free Medical books and a surprise gift. I understand that unless you hear from me, I will receive 6 superb new titles every month for just £2.99 each, postage and packing free. I am under no obligation to purchase any books and may cancel my subscription at any time. The free books and gift will be mine to keep in any case.

M8ZED

Ms/Mrs/Miss/Mr ............................................Initials .................................

BLOCK CAPITALS PLEASE

Surname .......................................................................................................

Address .......................................................................................................

...................................................................................................................

...................................................................Postcode...............................

**Send this whole page to:**
**UK: FREEPOST CN81, Croydon, CR9 3WZ**